W9-AWT-035

Other Books by Judy Delton

The Mystery
of the
Haunted Cabin

The
Mystery
of the
Haunted Cabin

Judy Delton

Illustrations by Anne Sibley O'Brien

Houghton Mifflin Company
Boston

Library of Congress Cataloging-in-Publication Data

Delton, Judy.
  The mystery of the haunted cabin.

  Summary: Three children spending the summer in an
old cottage on a lake try to track down the mystery of
a ghost who seems to be haunting the place.
  [1. Mystery and detective stories.   2. Vacations—
Fiction]   I. O'Brien, Anne Sibley, ill.   II. Title.
PZ7.D388Mzr 1986   [Fic]   86-7723
ISBN 0-395-41917-4

Text copyright © 1986 by Judy Delton
Illustrations © 1986 by Anne Sibley O'Brien

Printed in the United States of America

HAD 10 9 8 7 6 5 4 3

For Andrea Ozment, friend and editor

Contents

The Mystery
of the
Haunted Cabin

One

Summer Plans

It was June, and school was almost out. A long summer lay ahead. Barry Harrison could see days and days without much to do besides housework with his twelve-year-old sister, Robin, and long Scrabble games with his mother in the evening. (His father had died the year Barry was born, ten years before.)

His mother had just finished real estate school, and had a new job selling houses. She talked a lot about "escrow accounts" and "contracts for deed" and "liens," and she showed people large homes on Summit Avenue (in St. Paul, Minnesota, where the Harrisons lived) and small homes on lakes out in the country.

"I wish we could go on a vacation this summer," said Robin one evening. Their mother was still at work, and Barry and Robin were sitting on the front porch swing thinking about summer. "You know, somewhere like Disneyland or Monaco or Georgia." (Georgia was Robin's favorite place because it was Margaret Mitchell's home, and Margaret Mitchell had written her favorite book, *Gone With the Wind*.)

"Everyone at school is going somewhere," said Barry. "No one is just staying *here*."

"St. Paul could be fun," said Robin doubtfully. "I mean, we could dress up and give plays. We could charge admission and make money."

Barry had tried money-making schemes. They never worked. They always got him into some kind of trouble. And Robin was always wanting to dress up. Barry didn't like costumes, and he didn't like to "show off" in front of people, the way Robin did. Their mother said that Robin was a born actress and would be on the stage someday. "You were born for the stage," she would say about once a month.

"I don't want to be in a play," said Barry, thinking he'd better set her straight right away, while it was still spring. He didn't want her making any summer plans for the stage which included him.

"We'll go on long bike rides," she said. Robin was not easily discouraged.

"We do that all the time," said Barry.

Robin appeared to be deep in thought. "What we need," she said finally, "is Adventure."

Barry liked the sound of that word. He agreed; what they needed for the summer was Adventure!

"How do we get it?" he said. Robin was twelve years old and would know more than he did about that kind of thing, Barry thought.

"I've heard," she said wisely, "that it is all around us. We just have to look for it."

"Really?" said Barry. "There is Adventure in St. Paul?"

Robin shrugged her shoulders. "I don't know where, but I know if we pay attention it will come our way." Robin began to get goose bumps. That very often happened when she spoke. Her own voice reminded her of a fortuneteller she'd once seen on TV. It could be that she herself had psychic powers!

"Wow," said Barry. "I hope you're right."

"We have to watch and wait," she said, "and grasp

every opportunity that comes." Grasp. That was a fine word for a fortuneteller.

Barry was impressed. His sister might be flighty and scatterbrained, but she could be a lot of fun, and Barry liked her.

"Here comes Spencer," said Barry, looking down the sidewalk, where his friend was pedaling along trying to avoid the pedestrians in his path. Spencer's mother would not let him ride his bike in the street, even though it was against the law to ride on the sidewalk. His tires skidded to a stop on Barry's front lawn. He put down the kickstand and came to sit on the porch steps.

"What's new?" he said.

Barry wondered how anything could be "new" since he'd seen Spencer at school that afternoon. Robin wondered if Spencer's arrival could mean an opportunity for adventure. She doubted it. But everything had to be considered.

"Nothing's ever new around here," said Barry.

Spencer stretched out on the porch floor and made what appeared to be swimming strokes. "There's always something new," he said.

"Yeah, like what?" said Barry.

"Like the new trees they're planting in those cement tubs on Snelling Avenue," said Spencer, still swimming, "and the new mall that's going up in Midway Center. And the library is going to switch to summer hours next week. And the YMCA has this new handball class. I'm going to sign up." Spencer's face was red now, and he was running out of breath.

Barry and Robin sat on the swing and thought about what Spencer said. All those things were new. He was right. It didn't take much to get Spencer excited, however. Things excited him that were new but not necessarily Adventurous, they decided.

"I mean something *really* new," said Barry. "Something really exciting for us to do this summer. Better than handball."

"And better than Scrabble," added Robin.

Mrs. Harrison's car drove up the gravel driveway in the back yard. The car door slammed. Then they heard the key in the back door and shoes tapping across the floor and through the house to the front porch. The front door flew open, and two large multiple-listing books slid from under her arm to the floor with a thud.

"You'll never guess what I did today!" she said.

The three of them looked up at her without enthusiasm.

Mrs. Harrison waited with a cat-that-swallowed-the-canary look on her face. "Well?" she said.

"You sold a house," said Robin.

"You went to the grocery store," said Barry.

"You bought a new hat," said Spencer.

"No, no, and no!" said Mrs. Harrison. "Something better. I bought us a cabin on Horseshoe Lake! And we will go there to stay just as soon as school is out!"

Barry looked at Robin, and they knew they were thinking the same thing. Their watching and waiting had paid off sooner than they had thought! Adventure had come to them, and they were ready.

"See," said Spencer, "I told you there was something new!"

Barry and Robin were glad to admit that Spencer was right.

Two

Ready for Adventure

Barry and Robin followed their mother into the house. Spencer started home because his mother did not allow him out after dark.

Barry had mixed feelings about his mother's news. Why was she buying property when she was supposed to *sell* it? Where did she get the money? Still, whether or not she could afford it, there was no doubt about the fact that it meant ADVENTURE!

"It's an investment," said their mother, as if she knew they were wondering about the money. "It was such a good deal I couldn't pass it by! I'll use some of the money Aunt Elsie left us.

"Property is a sound hedge against inflation," she

went on. "We can always sell it if we need to. Meanwhile, we can have lots of FUN! We can fish and swim and hike and do lots of outdoor things together!"

"I can't wait to see it!" cried Robin. "Barry, Mom says there's a little beach house where we can give plays!" The prospect of a summer at Horseshoe Lake seemed more adventurous all the time.

"When can we leave?" said Robin. "When can we move in?"

"Well you have to finish school first . . ." said their mother. "Don't you?" Their mother liked excuses to keep them out of school.

"Of course!" said Barry. "We can't leave school early!"

"Some children do," said their mother thoughtfully. "Some parents take their children out early for trips to Europe and things . . ."

Barry sighed. "We have to finish school," he said firmly.

Robin pouted.

"It's only another week," he added. He was as anxious as Robin to get started on this adventure.

That night no one could sleep. Barry lay awake

thinking of the woods and nature and the unpredictable summer ahead. He thought about what clothes he'd pack and about the things he'd have to attend to, like the mail. It would have to be forwarded. And the grass would have to be cut at home, and the paper delivery stopped. He'd have to say goodbye to his friends — especially Spencer. He'd miss Spencer.

Robin thought only of adventure. She tossed and turned on her pillow, wanting the week to fly by. When she finally fell asleep she dreamed of buried pirate maps and new friends and their boat (they would have a boat, surely). In her dream, her family was shipwrecked on an island. She swam for help and saved Barry and her mother. She was given an award for bravery on the stage of the Orpheum Theater in St. Paul.

Mrs. Harrison thought about the wise investment she had made. Property always appreciated. One made money by investing wisely — especially in lake property. She pictured the sweeping green lawn that sloped gently down to the shore and the charming "vintage" cottage at the top of the hill. At least that was how the ad read: "Vintage lake home, with the charm of yesterday. Turn the key and move in . . ." The pictures had been a little hazy, but that was because of the shade in the woods. Ace Realty could be trusted. The other real estate agents who had become her friends had wanted the property themselves, but none of them could afford it. She would invite them up, once they were settled. They would have a barbecue on the beach! She wondered briefly if there was indoor plumbing, and how close the nearest neighbors were. It didn't matter. It was an investment, and it would be fun. That was the main thing. She closed her eyes and fell asleep.

All week long, Barry and Robin were busy preparing for the trip. Robin packed and repacked, changing her mind often about what to take.

"Will I need dressy clothes?" she asked her mother. "Or just jeans?"

"One never knows," said her mother. "We may be invited out to dinner — it may be a partylike community. It's best to be prepared. Better safe than sorry, my mother used to say."

Robin packed one sundress and the rest shorts, tops, and jeans. She took her makeup kit and her favorite books and the new pajamas she received for Christmas.

"Should we take blankets? Or sleeping bags?"

"Better safe than sorry," Mrs. Harrison repeated.

Barry packed flashlights and tools and his bankbook and fishing pole and swimsuit. He put in his drawing materials and bits of wire and string that came in handy around home; they were sure to be handy in the woods.

"Do the beds have sheets on them?" said Barry. "Or aren't there any beds?"

"Of course there are beds," said their mother in a positive voice. "Lake cottages come completely furnished with all the amenities."

Barry thought she sounded like an ad in the paper.

"Even dishes?" said Barry. "Shouldn't we take pots and pans to cook in?"

Their mother looked vague. "It's completely furnished, Barry. Just 'turn the key and move in,' the ad says."

"Didn't you notice when you were there if there were dishes and stuff in the cupboards?" said Barry,

putting his camping penknife, complete with cork-screw and scissors, into the corner of his bag.

Mrs. Harrison's face still had a vague expression. "Furnished is furnished," she said. "Ace Realty is a reliable company." Her voice trailed off as she started up the attic steps to look for her suitcase.

Barry wished he had been along on the initial visit. He would have looked things over and measured the property and checked the wiring and examined the cupboards and the foundation and the pipes. His mother probably didn't notice anything except the charm and the beach.

"How long will we stay?" Barry called up the attic steps after his mother.

"I thought you children would stay the whole summer," said his mother, from the top step. "I will drive back and forth every day to go to work. That way it will be a vacation for all of us, even though I'll be working."

It sounded too good to be true. Barry had a "feeling" for approaching trouble. A peaceful vacation, his mother driving home to lakeside dinners, evenings of sunsets over the water — all were things Barry could not see in store for his family.

"Barry?" said his mother, coming down the steps with her hair in disarray but with her suitcase in her hand, "Why don't you ask Spencer to come with us?"

It seemed like a great idea to take along a friend. Then Barry remembered: "Spencer's mother probably won't let him go. She worries about him."

Barry's mother frowned. "But I will be there. It isn't as if you were going to be alone at night. And Robin will be there all day to prepare your meals. It would be good for Spencer."

Barry had to admit that it *would* be good for Spencer to be away from home and the basic food groups and all that protein. And the fresh lake air was surely a selling point. But the fact that his mother would be there, thought Barry, probably wouldn't be an asset in Spencer's mother's mind. Barry's mother was not what might be thought of as the model mother. Still, it was worth a try. It would be fun to have Spencer at the lake with them! "I'll ask him," Barry said.

"Maybe Robin would like to bring a friend, too," said his mother thoughtfully.

"Peggy is going to camp when school's out," said

Robin when she was asked, "and Karen is going to Boston to her grandmother's for the summer. And there's no one else I want to be with all summer."

Barry stopped packing and ran over to Spencer's house to ask him if he could go. Spencer's eyes lit up with the promise of adventure, and he ran into the kitchen, where his mother was preparing bulgur wheat for salads, and asked her. Barry thought Mrs. Sims looked tired. She brightened at Spencer's words. She looked all ready to say, "Wonderful! I'll help you pack." But then her years of caution took over, and she said, "I don't know, Spencer . . . You could drown or trip on a tree root or eat too much sugar. And what if you get lost in the woods or step in poison ivy or get stung by a wasp?"

"They have doctors up there," said Barry quickly.

"Where *is* the lake, Barry?"

Barry was embarrassed to say he didn't know. "I'll call my mom and find out," he said. He quickly dialed the number. When he asked his mother the question, she hesitated.

"North," she said vaguely.

"But where?" said Barry. "Spencer's mother wants to know how far it is."

There was more silence. "Mom?" said Barry.

"It's just minutes away," said his mother.

"It's just minutes away," said Barry, hanging up the phone. He hoped Spencer's mother didn't ask any more questions. Maybe there *was* no doctor nearby. Maybe there was nothing nearby.

"Pleeeeease, Mom!" Spencer was saying. "Pleeeeease, can I go?" Spencer was folding his hands as if in prayer, and he had one knee on the floor.

"Well, it would be a fine chance for you to have a vacation, and for me to have a little time to myself," she said dreamily.

Probably she has never been away from Spencer since he was born, thought Barry. Even a great guy like Spencer could wear on you if you were with him nonstop for ten years!

Mrs. Sims had a faraway look in her eyes as she prepared the salads. "Well, all right!" she said. "I don't know if I'm doing the right thing, but we will try it. If Barry's mom is coming back and forth every day, you could always get home."

Spencer clasped his hands over his head and cheered. He jumped up and down all the way out of the kitchen. "Oh, wow!" he said. "I've got to pack!"

Barry told him what to bring and ran home to tell his mother that Spencer could come with them.

"Good," said Mrs. Harrison, looking at the road map. "Dear me," she said. "Our place really does appear to be in the north woods!"

Barry wondered why that surprised his mother. After all, she had bought it. Surely she knew where it was!

All week long, maps appeared on the tables and couches. And suitcases and boxes stood packed at the door to be put into the car at the last minute. At last school was out, the house was closed up, and the car was packed. Spencer came over bright and early on Saturday morning in a clean, crisp, white shirt and brand-new white sneakers.

The time had come at last. Everyone got into the car, and Mrs. Harrison, wearing her sunglasses, took her place behind the wheel, a Thermos of iced tea and three maps beside her.

Their summer of Adventure was about to begin!

Three

The Good Luck Lake

As the car wound its way north through the small Minnesota towns, Barry and Robin and Spencer watched the scenery carefully. They didn't want to miss a moment of this adventure.

"Pine City!" called Barry.

"Mora!" shouted Spencer.

They chattered away about the fun they would have fishing and swimming and exploring the woods. Gradually, as the ride went on, they talked less, and the rolling green hillsides with the white farmhouses began to blend into one long scene.

"Shouldn't we be there by now?" Robin demanded.

Her mother frowned. She pulled the car over to

the side of the road and studied one of the maps again. She looked puzzled.

"How far is it?" Robin went on.

"The ad said, 'Minutes from the Twin Cities,' " said Mrs. Harrison.

"In a *plane*," said Barry. "It's not minutes by car."

Mrs. Harrison took the paper with the ad in it out of her purse. "Drive minutes from the Twin Cities through lush countryside to your own lakeside cabin. Turn the key and move in." She put the paper down with finality, as if she had proved her words.

"Hours have minutes in them," said Spencer, looking at his watch. "We have been driving exactly one hundred and twenty minutes."

"That's a long drive for a commute," said Barry.

"And we aren't there yet," said Robin.

Mrs. Harrison stuffed the maps into the glove compartment and said, "I'm sure we are almost there." She started the car again.

"I have to go to the bathroom, please," said Spencer politely.

"It's time to stop for ice cream, anyway," said Barry's mother.

At the next town they stopped at a small restaurant that had ice cream and a bathroom and a man who knew where Horseshoe Lake was. He wrote the directions on a piece of scrap paper, saying, "Be sure to turn *right* at the KI Saloon, and not *left*." Everyone nodded. They could remember that.

"It's way out in the woods," said the man, waving his hand and shaking his head doubtfully.

"That's what we want!" said Mrs. Harrison, with feigned enthusiasm, Barry thought.

The man stood scratching his head as the car pulled away.

At the KI Saloon they turned right, and the pavement turned into a gravel road. A few miles farther along, it turned into a dirt road. Pine trees lined the sides of the road very closely, narrowing the road more and more the farther they went.

"Boy, are those trees *tall!*" said Spencer with a whistle. He leaned his head out of the window. "You can't even see the tops of them!"

"Virgin forest," said Barry's mother. "We are up in Paul Bunyan's woods, you know. Everything is bigger up here near Paul and his Blue Ox."

Barry had read about Paul Bunyan. He was a

giant lumberjack who used huge tree trunks for baseball bats.

"Is Paul Bunyan *real?*" asked Spencer.

"Of course," said Mrs. Harrison and Robin together.

"No," said Barry.

His mother and Robin believed in fairy tales and magic and make-believe. If Barry had not put an end to it, they would still believe in the Tooth Fairy and the Easter Bunny.

"He is too real," said Robin, getting in the last word.

The argument was forgotten because they all saw a sign by the side of the road that said Horseshoe Lake, with an arrow pointing to an even smaller road to the left. Barry's mother looked doubtful.

"It couldn't be on that road," she said.

"Well, did you go down this road last time?" demanded Barry. "Does this look like the road, or doesn't it?"

Then all of a sudden Barry knew. And Robin knew the same thing. They both glared at her and said in unison, very loudly, "You never were here!"

"There were pictures," said their mother. "I saw it all in pictures."

Barry was standing up in the back seat. "Pictures! You can't tell what a place is like from *pictures!*" He hit his forehead with the palm of his hand, just like Spencer always did. He slumped into the seat and said, "You bought a house without seeing it!"

"It could be ANYTHING," wailed Robin. "You could have bought a — a — *chicken house!*"

"A 'pig in a poke,' my mother calls it," said Spencer cheerfully. "That's buying something sight unseen," he explained to Barry.

"I did not buy a chicken house," said Barry's mother, with a slight pout. "I bought us a very nice vintage cottage."

Mrs. Harrison simply could not be trusted where business matters were concerned. There was no use being angry and impatient with her. It was her nature. She was impulsive and fickle. They would have to make the best of it.

The road became overgrown and rutted.

"Boy!" said Spencer. "It looks like no one has

ever been here before!" He leaned out the window in anticipation.

Spencer could afford to be excited. It wasn't *his* mother who had bought a pig in a poke. He could enjoy the fun and forget the problems.

Suddenly the children saw a flicker of light through the dark trees.

"The lake!" said Mrs. Harrison. "It's Horseshoe Lake!"

"I thought horseshoes brought good luck," said Robin. "This doesn't look like a lake that is good luck."

"Of course it is," said her mother. "It's going to bring us lots of good luck. Just you wait and see."

The road went almost to the lake, and then, just before the car plunged into the water, it turned abruptly to the left and went along the shore.

"No one has been here before," Spencer repeated. "We will be real pioneers, like Columbus!" Spencer liked the idea of being the first one to find a place.

The car bounced on and on through the wilderness.

"How will we know our house when we come to it?" said Robin.

"It will have an Ace Realty sign in front," said her mother.

Then someone *had* been here — to nail up a sign! The thought was reassuring to everyone but Spencer, who still wanted to be first.

They passed an old shed that had a hole in the roof and was leaning to one side.

"There it is!" said Spencer. "Is that your house?"

Mrs. Harrison looked as if she hoped it wasn't. "No," she said. "That is not our house. There is no sign in front."

Everyone was relieved to see that. Robin had her fingers crossed on both hands.

Barry wanted to ask what color the house was but decided he wouldn't. The fewer questions asked, the better. They would all know soon enough.

"I wonder if we have any neighbors," said Barry's mother. Robin, Barry, and Spencer were wondering that, too. It was very lonely here, even in the sunlight. What would it be like when dusk fell? There were no street lights here, as there were at home in St. Paul. And no telephones, probably. Just then, an animal ran in front of the car.

"Wow!" said Spencer. "That was a giant dog!"

"It wasn't a dog," said Mrs. Harrison. "It was a deer."

A deer. They were definitely in the country. It could have been a bear, Barry realized. He wished his mother had started out with something not quite so rustic. Something on the edge of the city, perhaps, like an apartment with a swimming pool. Buying a cabin so far away from everything was like jumping off a diving board without being able to swim. None of them were ready to "swim" in this wilderness without street lights or telephones — and with deer and bear at the back door instead of dogs and cats.

"Look!" said Robin, pointing up the road. "That's an Ace Realty sign!" Robin prided herself on her keen eyesight. Barry and Spencer leaned forward to look. Sure enough, there it was. Here in the middle of the virgin forest. Here where civilization had not yet struck. Mrs. Harrison's "wise investment."

The car pulled up into the tall grass behind the

"vintage cottage," and Mrs. Harrison turned off the engine. No one moved. The quiet was overwhelming. There wasn't a sound.

"Listen to that!" said Mrs. Harrison breathlessly.

"To what?" whispered Barry.

"The country," she said. "The lake. Nature."

They all nodded solemnly. It was the most Nature any of them had ever seen.

"You see?" said Mrs. Harrison. "What a wise, wise investment?"

Barry thought his mother was speaking a bit prematurely, since they were still in the car and had not yet seen the house.

No one made an attempt to open the door and get out. Mrs. Harrison said she wanted to "make the moment last," but Barry knew they all were afraid to go further.

"C'mon!" said Spencer, bounding out of the car and breaking the spell. He ran up to the cottage and looked into the window. Barry opened his door and cautiously walked around to the front (or was it the back?) of the house and looked at the lake. It was wonderfully blue, with soft ripples on the sur-

face. There were green pine trees along the shore-
line, and the blue, blue sky overhead was scattered
with fleecy white clouds. It looked like pictures of
heaven Barry had seen at Sunday school.

"You see? You see?" said his mother, coming up
behind him. "I told you it was a good buy."

Barry had to admit that even if this was all there
was, it would be a good buy. To wake up every
morning and look at this lake, and even swim and
fish in it, was worth lots.

"Now!" she said, taking a deep breath. "Let's
look at the house."

After fumbling with the key ring with ACE
REALTY — WE CARE on it, Mrs. Harrison finally
turned the key. The door opened, and they all saw
a large, old fieldstone fireplace and thirty-seven
small-paned windows letting sunshine in and giv-
ing a magnificent view of the water, trees, and sky.
It wasn't until they closed the door and were in the
house that they noticed the hole in the roof, the
missing cupboard door, and the bat hanging from
the rafter, and realized that there were no faucets
in the kitchen sink and no bathrooms at all.

"It will be like camping!" said Mrs. Harrison,

after going through the house a second time, just to make sure about the bathroom. "And we will get water from that pump in the front yard."

"I found the bathroom!" called Robin from somewhere outside. The others ran to find her.

"This is a *bathroom?*" said Spencer in surprise.

"It is an outhouse," said Mrs. Harrison. "For years this was the only kind of bathroom anyone had. We will live like pioneers in the wilderness. Isn't that an exciting thought?"

Spencer wasn't sure now about being a pioneer, but he was sure his mother would not approve of a toilet you could not flush.

The garage leaned a bit to one side, and the boat-house had mice. "We'll take care of that," said their mother, for the first time that day.

"I think," she said, "the first thing we should do is start to clean this place up. I'm glad I have two more days off so that we can get it into shape before I go back to work."

"What about soap?" said Barry. "And pails and rags?"

"I brought them," said Mrs. Harrison. "They're in that box in the trunk."

Barry was surprised that his mother had remembered practical things. He had underestimated her.

So after exploring the house and garage and boathouse and boat and the lakefront, they all got brushes and rags, and using water they had drawn from the pump and heated on the gas stove, they scrubbed everything in the house. They aired the beds and put sheets on them, and hung the blankets on the clothesline. Robin went into the woods and picked a big bouquet of wildflowers. She set them in the middle of the table in a peanut butter jar.

For supper they roasted the hot dogs they had brought with them over the flame on the gas stove, and by seven o'clock they were so tired from all the excitement and hard work that they collapsed on the beds and fell asleep.

The Harrisons slept soundly until the sound of sobbing woke Barry.

"Spencer?" said Barry, shaking him. "What's the matter?"

Spencer went on sobbing. "There isn't any," he said. "I looked all over, and there isn't even one."

"One what?" said Barry.

"One mailbox. My mom told me to be sure to write to her, and now there's no place to mail it."

By this time Barry's mother was awake, and she came and put her arm around Spencer. "I will take your letters with me when I go in to work," she said. "Don't worry about it. Your mother will get your letters."

Barry crawled back into his bed and listened to the water lapping the shore and the crickets chirping in the grass and the loon calling to its mate. (His mother had shown him the loon in the bird book she'd brought.) Before he had a chance to decide whether his mother had made a good or a bad decision, he was fast asleep.

Four

The Knock on the Door

The next day Barry's mother made a list of everything that needed fixing and said, "We'll do it slowly, one thing at a time, the worst things first. We'll look for a good repair person."

It reminded Barry of when they first bought the house in St. Paul. Why did their mother persist in buying houses that were old and decrepit — houses with sagging roofs and sloping floors and leaks where water and rodents could come in?

"Charm!" he could hear his mother say. "New things have no charm."

Barry and Spencer cleaned up the yard and hauled old trash away. They nailed a shingle over the hole in the roof, and they cut the grass. Robin and her mother measured the windows for curtains. And in between they rowed the boat on Horseshoe Lake and swam in the clear springfed water. Barry remembered seeing some lakes that were murky and muddy and full of weeds and couldn't help but feel that his mother had been just plain lucky with her unseen purchase. It could have been . . . Barry didn't want to think about what it *could* have been.

Mrs. Harrison's last two days of freedom sped by quickly, and soon it was time for her to start "commuting."

"It's a long drive every day," said Robin doubtfully.

"It will take a lot of gas," said Barry.

Their mother put some things in a bag and waved off their objections. She set the alarm for five A.M., and by five-thirty she was in the car starting the engine.

The children said goodbye, and Robin added, "We'll have dinner ready when you come home."

Barry said, "Don't forget to get bread and lettuce and eggs and milk," and then they all went back to bed. Five-thirty in the morning was very early.

By the time they got up at ten, it was raining. Dark clouds hung over the cottage, and they ate breakfast in gloomy silence. Robin burned the eggs, and the air in the house began to smell damp and musty and tinged with smoke. The children huddled together in front of the empty fieldstone fireplace. They felt cold and a bit melancholy.

"I wanted to go on a hike," said Robin with a pout.

"Maybe it will clear up this afternoon," said Barry. A loud clap of thunder swallowed his last words. Lightning lit up the cottage like sunlight for an instant, and then disappeared.

Then Spencer said those dreadful words, "It's a little lonely when it rains, isn't it?"

A little later he added, "What if lightning strikes us? Or a bear comes? Who would we go to for help?"

Those were things that Barry and Robin had thought of but had not said. They glared at Spencer for putting it out in the open where it seemed much worse.

"Let's play cards!" said Spencer, realizing his mistake and finding new strength now that they were worrying instead of him.

Barry shook his head. "I don't feel like games," he said.

Robin went into her bedroom and came out with a blanket wrapped around her.

"Charades!" said Spencer, holding up three fingers, rolling his eyes, and making chopping motions with his hands.

Barry felt angry that Spencer had worried them all and yet was acting as if everything was completely normal.

Robin paced the floor, watching the storm first from one window, then another.

"You know, this place isn't as big as it was yesterday," she said. "I mean, it's really a little cottage."

"It's the same size it always was," said Barry sensibly, though if he were being totally honest, he would have had to admit that the walls did seem closer together at the moment.

Spencer was working on the second word, first syllable, dancing around in front of them wordlessly. When he finally realized that he would not receive a response, he lost interest and began to wash the breakfast dishes.

"Hey!" he called from the kitchen, halfway through the chore. "Whose name begins with an *M?*"

Spencer walked into the living room with the dish towel wrapped around the silverware he was drying. He held up a damp fork. "Look," he said. "All the knives and forks and spoons have *M* on them. Your last name doesn't start with *M*."

"Everything came with the cottage," said Robin. "It wouldn't have our initials on it. It belonged to the people who owned it years ago."

Robin looked at the silverware. "It looks like real silver," she said. "Like sterling silver, not just metal."

Barry came closer to look. "It could be a *W*," he said, turning the fork around.

"It's an *M*," said Robin. "The people who used to own this place had a name that started with *M*." She looked out at the lake, thinking. "I wonder what their name was," she said, "and what happened to them."

"They probably died," said Spencer cheerfully. "They are probably dead and gone."

Robin shivered. It wasn't a good day to think about dying. It felt spooky here alone in the cottage in the rain with dead people's silverware. Robin couldn't forget about these unknown people whose name began with *M*. They kept coming back to her, and she wondered where they had come from and if they had children and what they were like. She wondered how they got here, so far out in the country, before cars . . . Did they have horses? And she wondered if they sat here on rainy days feeling lonely, and if they went fishing and hiking and exploring on sunny days, and if they lived in their cabin in the winter.

"Who do you think they were?" she asked Barry.

"Maybe farmers," said Barry. "Or fishermen. Or maybe they were like us. They just came for the summer."

"I'd like to know," said Robin. "I want to know who they were."

"Millions of names could start with *M*," said Barry. "Miller, Morgan, Magee, Michaels . . ."

After a while they grew tired of thinking of names and former owners, and Robin curled up in a chair with a book. Barry and Spencer played Old Maid and then Go Fish, until all of a sudden Robin looked at the clock on the mantel and said, "We have to think about what to cook for supper! Mom will be coming pretty soon!"

They immediately felt more cheerful, even though it was still dark and rainy out. Before long, Barry thought, Mom would be home, and they would have a nice hot dinner, perhaps with candles on the table, and she would tell them what had happened in town and what houses she had shown customers, and she would have brought all the supplies they needed. They would have a nice, warm, dry fire in the hearth, and they would all sit around it cozily, Mom knitting and Robin telling stories — even ghost stories. It would not be scary with their mother there and a bright fire burning. Then they would pop popcorn and play a game of Scrabble and finally crawl warm and cozy into their beds, where they would fall asleep listening to the patter of the rain on the roof. Yes, things felt better already, listening for the sound of a car coming up the dirt road.

Robin began to heat up the sauce that her mother had made for spaghetti. She buttered some garlic toast and set it in the oven, ready to be heated. And she put water in a pan to cook the spaghetti noodles. Barry and Spencer set the table with the monogrammed silverware and the old china plates from the cupboard.

"Look!" said Barry. "There is an *M* on the glasses, too!"

Sure enough, the water tumblers all had a very elaborate *M* engraved on them.

"I didn't notice that yesterday when we cleaned the cupboards!" said Robin.

Barry set the tumblers around the table, one at each place, for milk or water.

"If it wasn't so wet out, we could walk down the road and meet Mom!" he said.

"It's getting dark early," said Robin. "I don't think we should walk in the dark in the woods. If we got lost, no one could ever find us."

As it got later and later and darker and darker, Robin finished cooking the supper, and even heated the noodles and garlic toast. "She should be coming any minute now," said Robin, her face flushed from the hot stove.

Barry had turned the lamps on, and they cast a soft glow over the furniture in the rooms. Every

few minutes they looked out the window for the sight of headlights.

At nine o'clock, Robin said, "Maybe we'd better eat. We can save Mom her dinner and heat it in the oven."

"I think we should wait," said Barry. "She probably got into a lot of traffic on the highway out of town."

"Maybe she had some last-minute customers who wanted to see a house," said Robin.

"Or maybe she was in an accident," Spencer said. "Just a little one," he added, when he saw his friends glare at him.

Robin and Barry were thinking the same thing but had been afraid to say it. Their mother might be a little scatterbrained at times, but she was a reliable person. If she said she would be home for dinner, she would be. Her children could depend on her. So when she was this late, something had to be the matter.

The good feeling of anticipating her arrival had vanished, and the ominous feel of the rainy day was back. Robin served the spaghetti (a bit over-cooked) and the garlic toast (a bit burned), and there was only water to drink since Mrs. Harrison was to bring the milk. The trees outside bent with the wind, and a loose shutter banged on one of the bedroom windows. There were a lot of noises that were not the sound of a car driving up. They left the food untouched on their plates. Just as Barry said, "I wonder where she *is*," there was an extra-loud clap of thunder, and then all of the lights went out.

"YEOW!" shouted Spencer. "I can't see a single thing!"

"This is what they must mean by *pitch dark!*" said Barry.

"What is 'pitch,' anyway?" said Spencer.

No one answered. They could not see each other, or the lake. They could not see anything at all.

"Now, let's not panic," said Robin, who was never known for being sensible. But she was the oldest, so she couldn't afford to panic. "There are candles somewhere," she said. "I saw them this morning."

When a long streak of lightning lit up the house, Robin ran for the kitchen. She felt along the cupboard shelves until she came to the candles she had seen that morning. She reached over to the stove for a match and lit them. The three candles cast a meager, ghostly light across the room, wavering with some breeze in an eerie manner and playing shadows up and down the walls. Robin stood them in three of the glass tumblers with the *M* on them, and put one on the table and the others in the kitchen.

"Now if anyone has to go to the bathroom," she said, "They can take one of these candles along carefully."

The boys had forgotten about going out into the woods in the dark to the bathroom, alone. The longer they waited, the darker it would get, and the more scary. On the other hand, it was already pitch dark. There was no way it could get darker than pitch dark.

"I'll bet she got lost!" said Barry. "She never drove up here in the dark before. She probably took a wrong turn, and she had to turn around and go back."

"Then she should be coming any minute," said Robin. "She would stop to ask directions and be here anytime now."

"Unless," said Spencer, with his eyes wide in he candlelight, "there was no one to ask."

Barry scowled. He wanted to hit Spencer. Fight him. He was in the mood to fight. His adrenaline must be flowing freely, he thought. He'd have to control his emotions. It would never do to get in a fight out here in the woods. Spencer was his friend! All they had was each other. The three of them had to stick together. A fight out here in the wilderness could be like a forest fire — very destructive. Someone could get hurt, and there was no doctor around, that was for sure. He thought of how glibly he had assured Spencer's mother that medical aid was nearby. No, it would never do to wound Spencer, and have to admit to Spencer's mother that it was not true — there was no doctor around. He hoped they would never need a doctor, and Mrs. Sims would never know that she had let her son go off on a trip in this uncivilized part of the world.

"Now, listen!" said Barry. "We must stay together and protect each other."

"Well, why wouldn't we stay together?" scoffed

Robin. "I'm not about to go off on my own on a night like this!"

"There's nothing to be afraid of," said Spencer. "Just a little dark, and a little storm . . ."

Just then there was a loud knock on the back door, and Spencer ran to Barry and Robin like a shot from a gun. They huddled together in the corner of the living room and wondered what their next move should be.

Five

Alone in the Storm

"It's a burglar!" said Spencer.

"There are no burglars out *here!*" said Robin. "I think it must be a ghost."

"Ghost!" shrieked Barry, who was shivering down to his toes. "A ghost does not knock at a door. They come *through* doors!"

"Maybe it's someone selling something," said Spencer.

Barry supposed that anyone who thought there were mailboxes in the woods might think there were door-to-door salesmen, too. He was half cross with Spencer and half sympathetic. It wasn't his fault that his mother was overprotective. Spencer should have come to the woods gradually, Barry realized, not all at once right from the middle of the city. His mother should have sent him to camp, or let him go fishing, or at least let him ride his bike in the street before letting him loose in the woods. Barry felt himself growing angry with Spencer's mother.

"We need some weapons to defend ourselves," said Robin.

"No!" said Barry. "Someone might get hurt!" He had to see to it that there was no need for the nonexistent doctor.

"And it might be *us!*" shouted Robin, her voice lost in a clap of thunder. She reached out and picked up the small poker that hung by the fireplace.

"I think the salesman went away," whispered Spencer.

Just when they were ready to believe Spencer, the knock sounded again! Louder this time!

They leaped together again, with their arms around each other.

"We should have one of those things on the door so we could see out but they couldn't see in," said Robin. "Like in apartments."

"It's too dark to see even if we did!" said Barry.

"Let's hide," said Spencer.

The knocks were getting louder and more frequent.

Suddenly Barry surprised them all, including himself, by shouting, "Who's there?"

"I've got a message for you," said a strange voice. "Let me in."

"We can't let him *in!*" shouted Robin. "Mom would die if she knew we let a stranger *in.*"

It was true. Over and over she had warned them not to let anyone in the house whom they did not know.

"Let me in," the pounder repeated. "I've got a message for you."

Robin took the candle and walked bravely toward the door.

"We can't let you in, whoever you are, because we don't know who you are. You could be a criminal, or an escaped convict."

They could hear the man groan. The water was running off the roof and down his head.

"I have a message from your mother," he said.

At those words, Barry ran through the kitchen and threw open the door. The man did not look friendly. He looked wet and disheveled. He slid into a kitchen chair and wiped the water off his face. Spencer handed him a towel.

"I own the KI Saloon," the man said, "and your mother called there because it was the closest place to you she knew of." He shook his head as if she was wrong. "It isn't very close," he said. "You should have a telephone, you know."

"What about our mother? Where is she?" demanded Robin.

"Here's the message," he said, fishing in his pocket for a wet paper torn from a calendar. "I wrote down what she told me."

The words sounded like Mrs. Harrison's, but they came out of a strange man's mouth: " 'My darling children, the car broke down on the highway, and I had to be towed back to town. Ralph's Garage says it is the differential, and it will take a day to fix it. I will be there just as soon as it is mended. Please be brave and don't go into the woods or talk to any strangers, and I should be with you tomorrow night. I love you all very, very much, Mother.' "

Barry felt great relief that his mother was alive

and well but dismayed that they would be alone in the woods all night long.

"Would you like some spaghetti?" said Robin politely to the stranger. She was beginning to realize that it was no small thing to come through the woods in a storm to bring the news.

"No," said the man, standing up, and putting his wet cap on his head. "Just tell your mom to get you a phone."

"Thank you!" called Robin sweetly, as he set off with his lantern into the woods.

She slammed the door and locked it and said, "Well! That was just like *A Message to Garcia!* Through rain and fog and hail and dark of night to deliver a message!"

"That's the post office," said Spencer.

Barry nodded. "*A Message to Garcia* is about the one who didn't ask questions. He just got the message there, without looking for help."

"That is what this man did," said Robin. "He didn't look for help. He just came and delivered the message and saved the day."

"Night," corrected Barry.

Now that Barry knew that the knocker was no

one to fear, he felt relieved until he remembered that they were alone — and would be alone all night long. Robin and Spencer remembered the same thing, watching the flickering candlelight and hearing the wind whistling in the corners.

"I think we'd better all sleep together," said Barry. Robin and Spencer agreed. Robin went to the bedrooms and brought out blankets to spread on the living room floor.

"We'll sleep right here together, to protect each other," she said.

Robin piled up the blankets into three neat beds and put a pillow at the head of each. "Now," she said, "we may as well go to sleep. It is very late."

The three children did as Robin said. They lay down and pulled the blankets up around their chins. But no one felt like going to sleep. Barry's mind was spinning. His body felt tense, and he could not relax any of his muscles. An animal — maybe a coyote or wolf — howled in the distance. The wind whined in the trees. And there was a sort of crackling noise that sounded like something — or someone — walking through the brush in the woods.

"What's that?" said Spencer, sitting up.

The children listened. "Probably just an animal," said Robin.

Spencer's eyes grew large. "What kind?"

Robin had no idea what kind. "An otter, or a possum or a raccoon," she said. "Or maybe a deer."

Barry knew that Robin had no idea what animal was out there, or even if it was an animal! Instead of an animal, it could be a person. He wished he could believe Robin! The shutter began banging again. A clap of thunder rattled the windows.

Barry remembered his mother's words of only last week — "It will be a vacation for all of us!" — and thought how mistaken she was! This did not feel like a vacation to him. It felt like a nightmare. He wished he would wake up and find it was all a dream — the storm, the noises, being alone in the woods. But he knew it was real. Barry hoped his mother would learn something from this experience and not be swept away with emotion over a real estate ad again. One "Turn the key and move in" experience was enough.

Barry heard Robin breathing evenly. Could she be asleep? Was Spencer asleep, too? Was he the

only one awake to guard their lives against the fear-
some forces of nature? The candles had burned
down and gone out. It was so dark that when Barry
closed his eyes, there was no difference from when
they were open! It was like being blind! He would
have to depend on his sense of hearing and his sense
of touch to lead him.

He tried to think positive thoughts. If he could
only go to sleep, he would wake up in the morning
to the bright sunshine, and after a fun-filled day,
his mother would drive up — her arrival would
come before they knew it! The thought was con-
soling. Just get through the night, he told himself.

But down deep in his stomach, Barry felt that
more trouble lay ahead, before either the sunshine
came or his mother arrived. He turned his pillow
over and pounded it. When at last he fell asleep,
he had a fitful dream about a giant bear breaking
into the cabin, only to find that it was the man
from the KI Saloon dressed up in a bear suit to
frighten him.

Six

The Voice in the Night

Just when the bearman in Barry's dream was ready to grab him, Barry screamed loudly and woke up. Robin and Spencer leaped to their feet and scrambled to Barry's side.

"What was that?" shrieked Robin.

"It was me, yelling," said Barry, shaking from fright.

"No, listen!" she said. "Someone is shouting *outside!* That voice is coming from the woods!"

The three of them held on to each other and listened. Sure enough, there was an eerie voice that sounded as if it was borne along by the wind — a frail, unearthly voice that was saying, "Get off my property," over and over again.

Spencer threw back his head and howled. "It's the people whose name starts with *M!* They are calling from the grave — they want their house back!" he said.

"Get off my property," the voice called again.

"Does your name start with *M?*" quaked Spencer.

"Dead people don't talk," said Barry.

"Then they are alive!" shrieked Spencer. "That's even worse!"

"I've heard of spirits coming back to haunt the place they lived in," said Robin. "That sounds like a spirit voice. He must have gone to his grave leaving something unsettled," she said, rolling her eyes. "Or else," she added, "he was murdered here!"

They clung to each other in silence. There didn't seem to be anything to say or do except stay together.

"Get out!" the voice went on. "Get out. This is mine!"

"I think we should see where it's coming from," said Barry sensibly, even though his knees were shaking. He dragged the others slowly through the dark toward the back door.

"He'll get us!" said Spencer. "He doesn't sound friendly."

"Spirits can't harm us," said Barry. "They are harmless." Then he added, "I think."

Barry opened the back door just a crack. The voice was a little clearer. "You're strangers," it called, "on my land."

Mustering all of his courage, Barry called loudly, "Who are you?"

There was no answer. The spirit must have been surprised, thought Barry. He wasn't expecting someone to confront him. Maybe he would back off and go back to the spiritland he came from.

"Who are you?" repeated Barry.

"It's mine," called the voice. "Mine, mine, mine . . ." The word echoed through the wind.

"*M!*" shrieked Spencer. "I know it's that *M* guy! He's talking from the grave! Let's get out of here!"

"Get out, get out, get out . . ." the voice echoed.

The children listened to the voice rising and falling with the wind.

Gradually the voice got weaker and weaker and then faded altogether. The ghost appeared to be gone.

Barry closed the door with a shudder of relief.

"Maybe he'll get other spirits to help him," said Spencer, "and they will come back and drive us out."

"He's gone," said Robin. "I hope."

Barry was beginning to feel angry. The more angry he got about the spirit trying to take away their property, the less afraid he was. "It's our house," he said.

"Maybe Mom doesn't legally own it," said Robin. "Maybe she signed the wrong papers or something."

Barry didn't want to think about that. Knowing his mother, she could have blundered, and she might not have a legal claim.

"We'll find out as soon as she gets here," said Barry.

"You know what," said Spencer, who was still thinking about the letter *M*. "The *M* may not stand for his *last* name. It might be the ghost's first name! My mom has this big gold *N* that stands for Nora."

"But dishes belong to the whole *family*," said Robin. "You wouldn't put your first name on forks unless you were really selfish."

"*M* is his last name," agreed Barry.

Spencer wasn't about to give up his idea quickly. "I think his name is Max," said Spencer wisely.

Robin and Barry began to laugh. "Max!" they called, holding their sides. "Who ever heard of a ghost named Max!"

"What *is* a ghost name then?" said Spencer.

Barry had to admit he didn't know what name would be a ghost name. "But not Max, that's for sure," he said.

Laughing helped to give them courage. If you could laugh, thought Barry, things couldn't be that serious.

"I think we need to do some exploring," said Barry. "Maybe go to the city hall or somewhere to see if someone whose name starts with *M* really did live here once."

"There's no city hall around here," said Spencer, wise from his mailbox experience.

"There is in the nearest town," said Barry.

"We don't know where town is," said Robin.

Barry realized she was right. But he would think of something. The main thing was to try to get some sleep before morning. The sooner they did, the sooner the sun would make them feel better.

They all crawled under their blankets again, this time so tired that they all fell asleep immediately.

In what seemed like moments, Barry was awakened by the sound of sobs. They were coming from right beside him.

"Spencer?" he said. "What's the matter?" Barry reached over and shook him.

Spencer's pillow was wet with tears. "I want to go home!" he cried. "I want my mmmm-mother!"

Barry couldn't believe his ears. How could he go home now, in the middle of the night, without a car or any transportation?

"You'll be okay in the morning," said Barry. "Just lie down and —"

Spencer cried louder. "I don't want to wait till morning!" he said, shaking with sobs. "I want to go home now!"

Barry tried to console Spencer. He tried to think of what his mother would do in a case like this. She would probably make him warm milk and be kind and loving to him. But they had no milk, and Barry didn't know how to act like a mother.

"Do you want some water?" said Barry. "Or some leftover spaghetti?"

Spencer shook his head vigorously. He wiped his nose on the back of his hand and repeated, "I want my mom."

Barry sighed. Being nice wasn't working. He would have to be firm.

"You can't go home and that is that," said Barry. "Tomorrow my mom will come, and you can ride home with her the next day when she goes to work."

Spencer wailed. "I can't wait!" he said. "I'm homesick."

Barry had heard that being homesick was awful. He felt sorry for Spencer. By this time Robin was awake.

She rubbed her eyes and said, "What's the matter with Spencer?"

"He's homesick," said Barry. "He wants to go home."

Spencer started telling Robin that he had to go now, he had to leave, he had to see his mother. Nothing Robin said made him change his mind.

"All right," said Robin, standing up in the dark cabin. "Pack your things then, Spencer."

Spencer stopped crying and looked at Robin. She got another candle, lit it, and found Spencer's suitcase. She began to put his things into it. When it was packed, she handed it to him. She put her arm around him and led him to the back door.

The wind whipped into the cabin with the rain when she opened the door, and the woods loomed black as black could be.

Robin hugged Spencer and told him to be careful and not to step on any snakes and to say hello to his mother.

Spencer hesitated in the doorway. He took a few steps out into the rainy darkness, stood there, and then said, "Maybe I should wait till morning. It should be getting light before too long . . ."

"A good idea," said Robin, taking Spencer's arm and pulling him back in the house. "It will soon be light and it will probably stop raining."

Spencer crawled back under his blankets and Barry whispered to Robin, "Wow, that was taking a chance. What if Spencer really *left?*"

"I knew he wouldn't," she said, yawning.

Barry marveled at his sister's common sense. Was this the Robin he knew, the silly frivolous sister who was always fantasizing? What an unpredictable family they were turning out to be.

The children all slept, and when they woke up at ten o'clock in the morning, the sun was out and the birds were singing, and all thoughts of homesickness were gone.

"Let's explore!" said Spencer, bolting down the boiled eggs Robin made. "We can take these soda crackers along and see if we can find any clues to the voice and the *M* mystery!"

Spencer seemed to have forgotten entirely that he couldn't wait till morning and daylight to start home.

"Yes, let's explore!" agreed Robin, washing the dishes quickly while Barry dried them.

"I'm going to take along a paper and pencil to write down any clues, and a bag to put suspicious objects in," said Spencer. He ran to gather his equipment.

"I think we should examine the woods first to see if there is any sign of the voice, like footprints," said Robin.

"Spirits don't leave footprints," scoffed Spencer. "Only people leave footprints."

"Just the same," said Robin, "I want to see if there is any evidence."

"I'll catch up," said Barry, who wanted time to look around by himself.

After he finished drying the dishes, Barry brushed his teeth and went to sit on the front step to think. It was a perfect place to sit and think, with the warm sun pouring down on his head. The lake sparkled in front of him, and he could see the loon diving for fish. On the end of the old dock sat a mother duck and her babies, sun-bathing. The trees that had bent angrily in the wind the night before stood tall and gentle, their leaves barely rippling in the breeze. The beach house with its bright red roof leaned, Barry noticed, just a little to one side. Beside it, and in the middle of the front lawn, stood a flagpole without a flag.

"I'll bet that's what that clanging noise was last night!" said Barry, noticing the chain swinging back and forth alongside the pole. All of the noises seemed so harmless, even restful, during the day. But at night a fearful atmosphere took over.

Barry walked down to the dock and watched the water lap the old wooden boards. His mother would have to put this on her list of "things to repair" also. The boards were cracked and loose and someone could fall right through, into the water, thought Barry. *Unless it wasn't their property at all.* If the voice was right, they would not have any repair work to do. But why should he believe a ghost? Barry felt suddenly defensive about the property. He wanted it! He didn't want to give it up! His mother might make some rash decisions, but he would back her up.

Barry waded into the water, trying to forget morbid things like spirits and voices without bodies. The water was clear, and he could see to the bottom. Maybe he would find a bottle with a paper in it, solving this mystery. That is what happened in the mystery books he read. He looked along the beach for a bottle washed ashore with a message, but all he found were shiny pebbles, a few shells, and one dead fish.

After a while he lay down on the beach in the warm sand and tried to think about something else besides being haunted. Instead he fell asleep and dreamed that the ghost had a body. It had hold of him by the shoulders and was shaking him, demanding that they get off his property. Barry woke up suddenly to find Robin shaking him.

"You were really sound asleep!" she said. "You didn't hear us call you!"

Spencer stood over Barry, holding his "clue" bag. It was open, and Barry could see it was full of pinecones and rocks and porcupine quills and wildflowers, and one old plastic Frisbee.

"Did you find any clues?" said Barry to Robin, as he sat up and rubbed his eyes.

"A few," said Robin, mysteriously. "Like this old sock and this handkerchief," she added.

"We need *real* clues," scoffed Barry. "But I'm tired of ghosts and spooky stuff. This is our vacation. Let's swim!"

Robin and Spencer agreed. It was too nice out for spooky things. The voice felt more and more unreal under the bright sun. They all put on their suits and ran to the lake. It wasn't until late afternoon, when they had finished swimming and were lying on the beach, that Robin said, "I wonder if Mom would want us to swim all alone."

"We aren't alone," said Spencer, scratching his legs.

"I mean without an adult here," she replied.

"Well, we didn't drown, so there's nothing to worry about," said Barry sensibly.

Robin began to scratch her legs, too. When Barry stood up, he said, "Look! What is that all over you? And all over Spencer?"

Robin and Spencer looked at their legs. They were red and swollen. "Probably sunburn," said Spencer.

Robin looked closely and said, "That's not sunburn. It's not even. It's in blotches."

"Bugs!" said Spencer. "Something bit us!"

"I think," said Robin, "that Spencer and I got poison ivy in the woods."

Seven

Fishing

They had a lot to occupy their minds while they waited for Mrs. Harrison to come. Robin ran in to find the first aid kit they had packed, and came running out with a tube of ointment that listed poison ivy as one of the things it was good for. She smeared it gently on her legs and on Spencer's.

"We can't scratch it," she said. "Or it will spread like wildfire." She had heard her mother say that.

The rest of the day Barry stayed in the shade of the large pine trees and put sunburn lotion on his red skin. Robin and Spencer stayed in the cottage applying the ointment to their legs when they began to itch too badly. And finally, just before dark,

Mrs. Harrison's car drove up the dirt path to the house.

The three of them stumbled out to the car, red and swollen and stiff, and Mrs. Harrison threw her arms around them and said, "I didn't know WHAT to do when the car broke down. I worried and worried, and here you are, alive and well!"

In a few moments they assured her that they were alive, but far from well. She heard all about their nighttime adventures, and then she put water into a tub so that each of them could have a cool bath to soothe their hot skin. She made them cold lemonade and put a cold cloth on their foreheads. Then she cooked a good dinner with things they all liked, like corn on the cob. Barry had never seen his mother be so motherly. Perhaps mothering came late to some mothers, thought Barry, just as some children were called "late bloomers." His mother was just a late bloomer.

After supper the air cooled, and Mrs. Harrison built a fire in the fireplace with logs that Barry and Spencer brought in from the woods. The lights were on now, and once again the cottage was cozy and homelike. Robin, Barry, and Spencer almost forgot about the sunburn and poison ivy and spirit voices in the night.

"Mom, have you got the deed for this place?" said Barry, suddenly remembering the voice.

"Of course I do," said his mother.

"I think we should examine it," he said, "and see who the last owner was."

"That would be on the abstract," she said, going to get her briefcase. "But I bought the house from a family by the name of Finn. Charles Finn."

Barry looked at Robin and Spencer. "The voice must have been Mr. Finn's!" said Barry.

Barry put the house papers out on the table. They all looked at them together. Sure enough, the previous owner was Charles Finn!

"Finn doesn't start with *M*," said Spencer. "That voice was the *M* guy!"

"Maybe you just imagined that you heard a voice," said Mrs. Harrison thoughtfully.

Barry, Robin, and Spencer all shouted at once that they hadn't imagined it. "We all heard him, Mom," said Robin. She didn't want her mother to think that her overactive imagination was responsible for this.

"But if he is dead, he couldn't be talking," said Mrs. Harrison logically, "and if he is alive, he would have a body."

Barry, Robin, and Spencer nodded.

"I guess we will just have to wait until the middle of the night to see if the voice returns," she said.

They shuddered. But she was right again.

"And now it is time to get to bed."

Everyone was glad to go to bed. After the full day and sleepless night before, a good night's sleep would be welcome. It was only moments before they were all sound asleep.

Barry was the first one to hear the voice. At first he thought it was the wind in the trees. But no wind could sound that angry, and no wind could pronounce words!

"Get off my property!" the voice shouted, just as it had the night before.

Barry leaped out of bed and woke Spencer and Robin and his mother. They all went to the back door, Spencer with the fire poker, and opened it a crack. The voice was clearer now.

"This is my property! All of you, get off!"

"You see?" said Robin with a shiver. "It wasn't our imagination!"

Her mother agreed; this was indeed a real voice. "If we had a torch, we could see where the voice is coming from!"

Barry ran to get the flashlight. They shone it out the back door, but it only made a dim yellow light in the deep, dark woods.

"We can't go out in that dark woods!" whispered Barry. "We'd get lost."

"And we'd get more poison ivy," said Spencer.

"Maybe even murdered!" added Robin.

This time it was Robin who had said what everyone was thinking but no one wanted to say. "Lost" and "poison ivy" were horrible enough, but "murdered" was not something to say out loud.

The voice appeared to be coming from the woods, but Mrs. Harrison agreed that it would be very dangerous to try to find it in the dark. It kept repeating the order, in a louder and more angry voice.

"This is *my* property!" called Mrs. Harrison

finally, feeling defensive. "You should get off *my* property!"

The voice did not reply.

"Maybe you scared him," said Barry. "Maybe he is gone."

When there was no more response, Mrs. Harrison closed and locked the door.

Everyone went back to bed, but they tossed and turned all night long, thinking of the voice. By the time the sun came up, the family was sound asleep.

It was almost noon when they woke up. The sun was pouring into the windows. Mrs. Harrison had decided not to go in to the office but to do some work at home instead, and to try to help the children get to the bottom of the nighttime voice.

"What a fine day!" said Mrs. Harrison. "Surely nothing mysterious could happen on a sunny day like this!"

"Murder happens on sunny days," said Spencer in his usual cheerful way.

"No it doesn't," said Robin. "Murder is a night-time thing."

Robin and Spencer began to argue about the right time for murder, and Mrs. Harrison finally said,

"No murder is going to happen in the day *or* night! I am going to do some investigating myself today."

After a very late breakfast, Mrs. Harrison went off to the KI Saloon to ask some questions about ghosts in the neighborhood, and Barry, Spencer, and Robin decided to go fishing. It was hard to stay in the mood for mystery when the sun was shining and the lake was so blue. Barry had read magazines and books about fishing tackle and hooks and lures and sinkers, and he acted as the leader. Robin and Spencer put more ointment on their poison ivy, and they all headed down to the shore.

Barry and Spencer lowered the rowboat into the lake. Barry dug a hole and found some worms, which he put into an old tin can. "The book doesn't say how squirmy these things are!" he said.

"Now, I don't know how to row too well, so we will stay close to shore," he continued.

"Good," said Robin. "I don't trust these life preservers. They look like plain, ordinary pillows."

Barry baited all the hooks. By the time he had one done, another was ready to be baited again.

"Where is my worm going?" cried Spencer.

"The fish are nibbling it without getting caught," said Barry. He barely had time to put his own hook in the water because it took so long to keep Robin's and Spencer's hooks supplied with the slippery worms.

Once all three hooks were in the water, Barry had time to look out at the lake. It was so blue and clear that if he looked down, he could see almost to the bottom. It was hard to believe that this was the same lake that thunder and lightning had ravaged so recently. Now the only noise was the lap-lapping of the water against the boat and the faraway call of the loon.

As they fished, Spencer chattered away about ghosts and monograms and haunted houses. "It's like Halloween every night here!" he said excitedly.

"My book says that talking frightens fish away," said Barry. "The reason we are not catching anything is that you are talking, Spencer."

Spencer had a hard time not talking. "How do we know when we have a fish?" he said. "Maybe there is a fish on one of our lines right now!"

"Your bobber will go down into the water, and

you will feel a jerk on the line," said Barry knowledgeably. "You have to watch that bobber."

They all sat quietly and watched the bobbers.

"I wonder who will catch the first fish," said Spencer in a whisper.

"I know the most about fishing," said Barry. "It seems only right that I'd catch the most. Or at least the first one."

"The fish don't know that you know the most," said Spencer.

Barry put a new worm on Robin's hook. As soon as she tossed it back into the water, the bobber disappeared, and her pole bent in half.

"Something is on my line!" she cried.

"Of course there is!" said Spencer, jumping up and down and making the boat rock. "That is what we are here for, to catch fish!"

"Sit down!" shouted Barry. "Don't ever jump up in a boat, Spencer. You could tip us over, and we could drown."

"Jerk the line," Barry called to Robin. "That sets the hook in his mouth, the book says."

Robin jerked the line. Something definitely was

on her line. It swam in circles around the boat trying to get away.

Barry and Spencer reached over and helped her pull the fish in. It flopped on the floor of the boat, at their feet.

"Wow!" said Spencer. "That is a big fish!"

"It doesn't look like a sunny or a bluegill," admitted Barry. Barry was disappointed that he, the only fisherman in the group, had not caught the first fish. It was embarrassing. On top of that, this *was* a big fish. He had not really believed any of them would catch this big a fish with just a little worm.

Barry put on the canvas gloves he had brought and picked up the fish. He had to use both hands. He had to have Spencer help him hold it while he wiggled the hook to get it out of the fish's mouth. Finally it came loose, and they managed to drop the fish in the pail they had brought along for that purpose.

Barry hung the pail over the side of the boat on a piece of rope. Then he paged through the wet magazine he had along with him. He looked at the fish and then at the pictures on the page.

"I think it is a walleye!" he said. "Those are the biggest fish in Horseshoe Lake!" Barry looked into the lake for weeds. The magazine said they were found in weeded areas.

"Fishing is more fun than I thought!" said Robin. "I'll bet I can bait my own hook if I wear those gloves!"

"Go ahead," muttered Barry. The reason he hadn't caught a fish was that he was so busy teaching them about fishing and taking care of their lines, he thought.

Before long, Robin caught another fish. Then another. After that, Spencer caught a fish. Barry was the only one who had not caught a fish.

He put his line out over the side of the boat. Then he took the worm off and put on a plastic minnow. Still he didn't catch a fish.

Another boat passed them on the lake. It had a motor and was moving very slowly. The motor made ripples in the lake, and the Harrisons' boat began to rock gently. Barry wondered if the people in the other boat had any fish. Just as he sat wondering that, something very heavy pulled his line.

"Help!" he called to Spencer and Robin. Spencer forgot he should not stand up in a boat and stepped over the seat to help him. As he did this, his arm bumped one of the oars, and the oar bumped the pail holding the fish. The rope broke, and the pail fell into the lake. As the children watched, their fish, including Robin's big walleye, swam away. The pail bobbed up and down on the lake, just beyond their reach!

At the same time, Barry let go of his fishing pole, and it flew into the water.

"My one chance to catch a fish," cried Barry, "and I missed it."

"You didn't miss it, Barry," said Spencer. "No one could hold on to a pole with a fish that size on it! It bent the pole right in half! That must have been a giant fish!"

Barry watched his pole sink. He could barely make something out at the end of the line. It did not look like a fish. It looked more like someone's old rubber boot. But he wasn't sure of that. He could not see for *sure* that it was not a giant fish.

"Wow!" said Robin. "Yours must have been the biggest fish of all. And it got away."

Barry wondered if they knew it was not a fish

and were just pretending in order to make him feel better. It seemed as if they were sincere. And who knew — it could have been a fish.

"All our fish are gone," said Spencer sadly. "They all got away."

Somehow the catastrophe had cheered Barry. He was no longer the only one without a fish. He packed up the fishing tackle and supplies and began to row to shore. As they drew closer, they could see Mrs. Harrison on the shore waving to them. She must have returned from her investigation at the KI Saloon. And she was probably planning on fish for supper that night.

That reminded Barry of something. Fish did not go from the lake into the frying pan. Fish had to be *cleaned and scaled!* As far as he knew, his mother could not clean fish, and he and Robin and Spencer surely could not! Thank goodness for that old boot (or giant fish). If it had not been for his large "catch," the pail of fish would not have spilled, and they all would be faced with the task of having to clean them!

"What's Mom saying?" said Robin. "I can't hear her."

Mrs. Harrison was calling something in an excited voice from shore, but her voice was blowing away on the breeze.

"She's probably asking if we caught any fish," said Barry.

Spencer shook his head. "No," he said. "What she is saying is, 'We are going to talk to our ghost, children! We are going to have a seance tonight!' What's a seance, Barry?"

Eight

The Seance

As Barry rowed the boat closer to shore, they all could hear Mrs. Harrison's excited words.

"Hurry!" she called to them. "I have so much to tell you!"

"We have a lot to tell you, too!" called Robin.

Barry gave the oars one last pull, and the boat hit the shore. Robin and Spencer jumped out and pulled it up onto the beach where it would not drift out onto the lake. Barry gathered the fishing equipment together and carried it to the boathouse. Spencer told Mrs. Harrison excitedly about the fish that got away.

"All of them?" she said in a surprised voice. "They all got away?"

Spencer reenacted the scene in the boat when Barry's pole caught something so big that it bent in half and then fell into the lake, dislodging the pail of fish hanging from the side.

"Crash!" said Spencer, winding up the tale. "Everything fell in the lake!"

Mrs. Harrison waited politely to be sure that they had finished their fishing stories, and then said, "Well, I have some news, too!"

Everyone sat down on the lawn chairs in the front yard to listen.

"Well," she began. "I went to the KI Saloon to do a little investigating about our ghost, and guess what I found out?"

This time the three of them waited politely.

"At first no one would tell me anything, but I kept asking questions," said Mrs. Harrison.

"Just like a real detective," said Spencer, impressed with his friends' mother.

"I said, 'Do any of you know Charles Finn?' and the funniest look came over everyone's faces, like they knew plenty but wouldn't say anything. Why, Mr. Finn could have been sitting there that minute!"

"Was he? Was he?" asked Robin.

"I don't think so," their mother went on. "I said, 'Well, we live in his cabin, and we are hearing voices at night, telling us to get off his land. I want to find out who it is.' That's what I told them. And you will never guess what they said."

"*Tell us!*" they shouted.

"They said," Mrs. Harrison went on mysteriously, "that there is a curse on this land! They said our cabin is haunted! And they finally told me that *that is why Charles Finn sold the property!*"

"Ace Realty should have told us it was haunted," muttered Barry. "People don't want to buy land with a curse on it."

"They didn't know," said their mother. "Mr. Finn didn't tell them why he wanted to sell."

"Wow!" said Spencer. "Really, truly haunted."

"Well," said Robin. "We *know* that. That is really no news. What we need to find out is who is haunting it."

"That," said their mother, "is exactly what we are going to do tonight at midnight."

"How?" said Spencer, with his eyes open wide.

"We will get in touch with the spirit on the other

side," said their mother, "the one who is haunting us. If it is not Charles Finn, then it must be someone who lived here many years ago — maybe even in another life. We must communicate with him, with his soul," she said softly.

Barry shuddered. It sounded like a very spooky business.

"Maybe we should just sell this place and forget all about it," he said.

"Sell it?" said Spencer. "You can't *sell* it! You have to *solve* it!" He was into the spirit of intrigue now.

"Do you mean we have to talk to someone who is — *dead?*" shrieked Robin.

Her mother nodded, rolling her eyes eerily.

"When people are dead, they can't talk," said Barry.

"This ghost does," added Spencer. "And ghosts are all dead."

"There is a special way of talking to spirits," said Mrs. Harrison. "Under certain conditions, we can communicate with them. We will contact this spirit and ask him to leave — in a nice way, of course. We wouldn't want any hard feelings."

"We might get him mad at us, and then he might do something awful," said Barry.

"How do we do it?" said Spencer anxiously. "When do we start?"

"We will have a seance," said Mrs. Harrison. "But we can't do it till midnight. That is the hour the spirits are most . . . available."

Robin got involved in the idea quickly and said, "What do we need? Do we need special clothes or a telephone or what?"

Barry couldn't believe how gullible his sister was. "You can't really call ghosts!" he said.

"Of course you can," said his mother. "Why, they do it in movies and books all the time."

Barry looked doubtful.

"We have to meet this spirit on his own ground," she added. "Now we will need to move the table into the middle of the living room . . . and we'll need a tablecloth and a candle . . ."

Robin ran off to look for a tablecloth.

"I know where the candle is!" shouted Spencer, remembering the candlelight during the storm.

"Barry, you take one end of the table and I'll take the other," said his mother.

"Why can't it just stay over here?" said Barry.

"We have to sit in a circle around it," said his mother. "Someone on each side. It needs to be in the middle of the room."

Barry helped his mother lift and drag and slide the table across the floor.

"This is dumb," he said. But even as he said the words, he began to be swept up in the excitement. He also felt some fear that his mother might be right, and that they might really be able to talk to the ghost. And that felt downright spooky. The day school was out, he had said that he wanted adventure! It looked as if they were all getting plenty of that this summer at Horseshoe Lake!

"I can't find a tablecloth," called Robin. "But I found this old sheet — I'll bet spirits don't know the difference between a tablecloth and a sheet."

Her mother frowned. "It has to look authentic," she said.

Robin spread the sheet neatly on the table. Spencer set the candle in the middle of the table.

"What else do we need?" said Robin.

"We just have to wait until midnight," said Mrs.

Harrison. "Maybe we can play Scrabble and pop popcorn. First we should have some supper."

No one seemed to be hungry, so Mrs. Harrison put out some carrot sticks and some fruit and cheese to nibble on.

"I'm tired," said Barry. "I feel like going to bed." The fresh air on the lake had tired all of them.

"Why don't we take a nap, and I will set the alarm clock for twelve o'clock midnight," said Mrs. Harrison.

Spencer admitted that he might be able to use a nap.

Everyone got ready for bed, even though the sun was just setting. Once in bed, though, no one could sleep. They all thought about the seance and the possibility of identifying their ghost, and maybe even talking with him! The thought of that, plus the sound of the night noises, kept each of them from relaxing.

The sounds were especially ghostlike this night, Barry thought. From his window, he could see a full moon over the lake. Wasn't a full moon when bewitching things happened? A time when wolves howled, and even dogs? Murders were committed beneath full moons, and Halloween witches wearing pointed hats and black capes rode broomsticks in front of them. A full moon was spooky. If ever there was a good time to talk to a ghost, this would be it.

Barry lay and listened to Spencer toss in his bed. He could hear Robin going into the kitchen for something to eat. How could she eat on a night like this? Even his mother had her light on and couldn't sleep.

After what seemed like ages, Barry fell asleep and dreamed that their ghost came out of the woods, wearing the sheet Robin had put on the table, and sat down at the seance with them. Barry kept telling him, "You are supposed to be on the other side! In another world! You are a spirit!" It seemed that the ghost did not know the first thing about a seance. He came toward Barry with his spiritlike arms out and touched Barry's shoulder.

"No! No!" He was shouting as he woke up to find his mother shaking him by the shoulders.

"You were dreaming," she said. "And it is time to see if we can contact the ghost."

Barry couldn't think of anything he wanted to do less than meet that ghost.

"Come on!" called his mother, waking Robin and Spencer, who had finally dropped off to sleep.

The three of them followed Mrs. Harrison (who appeared to be wide awake in the middle of the night), rubbing their eyes and feeling groggy. It reminded Barry somewhat of all the Christmas Eves when they'd been awakened after Santa left to open presents. But it was not like Christmas for long. They got to the living room and sat at the table, one on each side, facing each other. Mrs. Harrison lit the candle. Then she turned out all the other lights in the house.

"Boy is it *dark!*" said Spencer with a whistle.

The candlelight wavered in front of them, making strange shadows on the sheet and on the walls around them. They looked like figures moving slowly back and forth.

"Now we will all hold hands under the table," said Mrs. Harrison. "We will think very hard about the ghost, and we will try to get his attention. I have heard that if he is near, the table will begin to rise in the air."

"Rise in the air?" said Barry, feeling his hair rise on end as he said it. "How can that happen?" Barry read his science magazine every month and had never heard that this was possible.

"Supernatural," said Spencer quietly.

The four sat around the draped table holding hands, when all at once Mrs. Harrison sent shivers down their spines by saying in low tones, "Is the spirit who haunts our house out there? Will he please come forward and make himself known?"

A breeze seemed to come from somewhere, even though all of the windows were closed, and shadows danced on the walls — large shadows, from only a small candle flame!

After a few moments their mother repeated (more impatiently, Barry thought), "Will the spirit who has passed over and come back to haunt us come forth and tell us what he wants?"

Suddenly Robin began to giggle. "It sounds like the voice on the loudspeaker when a little kid is lost in the mall," she said.

Barry could feel his mother frowning in the darkness. "This is serious business," she whispered. But it was too late. Robin's laughter had

infected Barry and Spencer, and the more they tried to be serious the more they laughed.

"You've broken the spell," Mrs. Harrison said accusingly. "Now we will not be able to locate him."

All of a sudden a gust of wind blew the cabin door open, and a voice said, "Get out! Get out of here! This is *my* land!"

The children turned white and forgot that anything had been funny.

Mrs. Harrison said, "It's him! He came after all! Hold hands and communicate with him!

"Oh, spirit of Horseshoe Lake, tell us who you are, and why you are not at peace!"

"Get out!" answered the spirit. "Get off my land!"

"It is our land," explained Mrs. Harrison, as if she was reasoning with a clerk in a department store instead of a ghost. "We purchased it from Ace Realty and Charles Finn, and I can show you the deed to prove it."

The ghost's voice faded away, just as it had the other nights.

"Wait!" shouted Mrs. Harrison. "Come back! Tell us who you are and what you want!"

There was nothing now but the sound of the wind in the trees.

"Darn!" said Mrs. Harrison crossly. "Just when we had him here in our midst."

"We didn't have him here!" said Barry. "That was the voice we heard the other two nights — the voice in the woods."

"The *M* guy!" said Spencer. "It's that *M* guy back again."

Mrs. Harrison shook her head. "It was the spirit we brought forth at our seance," she said. "We summoned him forth, and he came."

Barry and Spencer were standing now, trying to convince Mrs. Harrison that no ghost had come into the room.

"What's the difference?" said Robin. "It's the same guy anyway, whether he's in the woods or in the seance. I'm tired."

Robin yawned and started for bed. Her mother followed, saying, "Next time he will respond! He disappeared just a little too soon . . ."

Barry and Spencer blew out the candle and went to bed. "I think it is up to us," said Barry confidentially. "I think it is up to us to solve the mystery on our own."

Spencer agreed. "All we need is some more clues," he said. "We'll find them tomorrow."

Nine

Christmas in Summer

But the morning after the seance, no one felt like looking for clues. They felt tired and cross, and everyone overslept, which made Mrs. Harrison late for work. Instead of looking for clues, they did the chores that Mrs. Harrison had listed on the refrigerator note pad, and then they went back to bed for naps. When they got up again they played charades and then a game of Scrabble, and by that time Barry's mother was home from work, and everyone was in a better mood. Mrs. Harrison told them about her weekend plans.

"We are going to take pictures!" she said. "I want to take pictures of all of us for our Christmas cards."

"It's the middle of summer, Mom!" said Barry.

"That's the best time," she replied. "That way we can have our lake and cottage in the picture. And when the holidays come, we will have the pictures all ready to send to the card company. No last-minute rush!"

"I don't feel like Christmas," sulked Robin.

"I brought some Christmas records to set the holiday mood," said her mother, going to her room and coming out with *A Christmas Sing-Along* and *White Christmas*, recorded by Bing Crosby. She turned on the old phonograph in the living room and put one on. Soon peals of Christmas music flowed through the cottage.

Spencer began to sing. He picked up the spirit of things quickly.

Mrs. Harrison was lost in her plan. "We'll hang some stockings on the fireplace tomorrow, and we'll take some pictures of you and Robin and Spencer in your sweaters looking to see what Santa left," she said. "And then maybe one of all of you decorating that fir tree on the front lawn. We'll string popcorn and make ornaments, and it will be very festive!"

That night Barry dreamed of holly and mistletoe

and a large red stocking with his name on it. When he looked inside, it contained a ten-pound walleye.

The next morning, Barry, Spencer, and Robin awoke to strains of "Silver Bells," and four bulging stockings were hanging on the mantel. Mrs. Harrison was stringing popcorn in the kitchen. Barry thought he could smell pine.

Mrs. Harrison handed them each a pair of scissors and some colored paper. "We have to make ornaments," she said, "and decorations for the walls."

The children cut and pasted all morning. Barry cut fish out of red paper, and Spencer cut out a large black boot.

"What's that for?" said Barry, wondering if Spencer had seen the boot on the end of his fishing pole, after all.

"It's Santa's boot," said Spencer.

Barry felt relieved. He was getting touchy about his fishing skills.

By noon the temperature had risen to eighty-five degrees. Mrs. Harrison wiped her forehead with her handkerchief, and Barry poured iced soda pop for them to drink as they worked.

"Boy, this is the warmest Christmas I can remember!" said Spencer jokingly.

"Perhaps we should all put on our bathing suits before we go out to trim the fir tree," said Mrs. Harrison.

Soon everyone had on swimsuits, and before they began to trim the tree, they took a cool swim in the lake. Mrs. Harrison set up the stepladder beside the tree and began to string tiny colored lights around its branches. The children hung the ornaments and decorations on the branches, while Spencer climbed up the ladder to put a star at the very top.

They stood back and looked at their work.

"We need snow," said Robin. "There should not be green grass underneath the tree."

"Snow would melt fast on a day like this," said Spencer. "That is, if we had some."

"We need fake snow," said Mrs. Harrison, thinking.

"Soap flakes!" said Robin. "Soap flakes look like snow, and they won't melt!"

She ran to the kitchen sink and came back with a large box of Sudsy Snow soap powder.

"I could sprinkle the snow over the tree from the top of the ladder as you take the picture," said Spencer. "It would look as if it was snowing!"

"Snow in the background!" said Robin. "That's a good idea!"

Her mother frowned. "I don't think we need to make it snow," she said. "I think we just need a little on the branches for effect, and maybe a little underneath the tree."

After the snow was in place, Mrs. Harrison shouted, "Get your sweaters on! It's time for the pictures!"

Her camera was set up on a tripod, and she focused the lens on the tree.

"We'll roast in sweaters!" complained Robin. "We'll just wear our bathing suits with scarves around our necks."

"A bathing suit does not look like Christmas," said her mother. "We can't have snow and evergreens and bathing suits all in one picture. It would confuse people."

The children reluctantly pulled ski sweaters over their heads, as the temperature rose on the thermometer to ninety degrees. Beads of perspiration stood out on their foreheads, and Spencer's face turned bright red.

"You look like you are all red and rosy with the cold!" said Mrs. Harrison.

"We are red and rosy from the heat," grumbled Barry from under his tassel cap.

Mrs. Harrison quickly snapped some pictures around the tree with her other camera, a Polaroid. The children gathered around to see them as they came to life in full color.

There there were, the three of them dressed in bright wools, in front of a snowy tree with twinkling colored lights.

But in the background, right behind this winter scene, was a rippling blue lake with a sailboat lazing on the surface, bobbing up and down in the summer sun.

"The lake!" shouted Barry. "The lake isn't frozen!"

"And a sailboat," laughed Robin. "Mom is right — people are going to be confused."

"It's a good picture," said Mrs. Harrison thoughtfully. "It would be different from other cards people receive at Christmas . . ."

"Ho!" said Barry. "It would be different all right!"

"It would be unforgettable," Mrs. Harrison went on. "A memorable Christmas card."

"It would be a conversation piece," said Robin, remembering some unusual objects at a friend's house that were called that.

"We will use it," said their mother. "And now we will take some others around the fireplace."

Mrs. Harrison moved her camera equipment into the house, and the children gathered in front of the fireplace.

"Smile now, like it really is Christmas!" she said.

Mrs. Harrison took six pictures of Barry, Spencer, and Robin in front of the fireplace, and then some more of Barry and Robin outside, this time tossing make-believe soap flake snowballs at each other. Finally she said, "I think we have enough now. You can take off your sweaters."

She folded her tripod and put the camera away as the children pulled off their sweaters.

"I wish we had presents to open," pouted Robin after another swim. "What is Christmas without presents?"

"I'm afraid I didn't think of that," admitted her

mother. "But I can make us a fine Christmas dinner. I have a chicken that I will stuff with dressing,
and we will pretend it is a turkey."

"Good!" said Spencer, who liked to eat.

That night at dinner, Barry announced, "Tomorrow, we are going to look for more clues to our
mystery of the ghost."

"Fine!" said his mother, holding up her glass of
iced tea. "I'll toast to your good luck, and a merry,
merry Christmas!"

"God bless us everyone," said Spencer, holding
up his glass of cold milk.

"And happy new year!" said Robin, beginning a
chorus of "Auld Lang Syne."

Soon all four of them, still wearing their swimsuits, were singing holiday songs around the cold
fireplace. Then it was time for bed, and Barry fell
asleep with dreams of sugar plums and ghostly clues
dancing in his head.

Ten

More Clues

The next morning dawned bright and sunny, and Mrs. Harrison left for work with a sandwich made of leftovers from the Christmas dinner. When the children got up, they cleared the last of the holiday away and got ready to spend the day looking for clues to the mystery.

"Where will we look?" said Spencer. "Where do we look for clues?"

"If we knew, we wouldn't have to look," said Barry sensibly. "We have to look everywhere, Spencer, till we find what we want."

"What do we want?" asked Robin. "What are we looking for?"

Barry sighed. "We are looking for a clue to tell us who the ghost is."

"It's the *M* guy," said Spencer. "We already know that."

"We are not positive," said Barry. "And we don't know who he is or where his voice is coming from."

Robin and Spencer had to admit he was right. There were many things they did not know.

"But when we do find him," said Spencer wisely, "his last name will begin with *M*, mark my words."

"We won't know till we find him," said Barry.

"Do we have a magnifying glass?" said Spencer. "And a pair of binoculars?"

Barry shook his head. "Of course not," he said. "We don't have stuff like that up here. And anyway, we don't need them."

"Yes we do," said Spencer. "We need equipment to find things."

Robin was searching around the kitchen and came out with a big brown grocery bag. "This is for clues," she said.

Spencer went to the garage and got an old pail and shovel (in case they had to dig for clues), and

Robin carried her bag, and Barry went empty-handed. They set off through the woods in the direction the voice had come from.

"Boy, it's dark in here!" said Spencer, when they had not gone very far. The tall pines surrounded them, and it didn't look as if anyone had ever walked there before.

"What if we get lost?" whispered Robin. "I've heard of children like Hansel and Gretel who wandered off and lost their way back. All the directions look the same."

"We need some white pebbles," said Spencer. "We should have left a trail of pebbles."

"We can tell the direction by the setting sun," said Barry, pointing. "It comes up in the east, and at noon it will be overhead, and in the evening it will set in the west."

Robin and Spencer stared at Barry with respect. His statement made a lot of sense. You couldn't get lost if you knew directions.

Or could you?

"What good does it do to know where the sun sets?" said Robin. "Which way is our cabin? That is what we have to know."

Barry had to admit he was not sure what direction the cabin was in. "We won't get lost," he said confidently. "It is broad daylight."

It did not look like broad daylight in the woods, and the brush and fallen trees and undergrowth were so deep that it was difficult to walk.

"What is that smell?" said Spencer, stopping for a moment. "It smells like . . . Christmas!" Spencer had Christmas on his mind.

"It's pine," said Robin. "These are all pine trees."

The children all sniffed the air. "It smells good," said Barry. As they stood sniffing, they noticed that they did not hear a single sound. It was perfectly quiet. Not even the breeze could reach them beneath the tall trees.

"It's just the place for a ghost to live," Spencer said softly.

All three of them shuddered. This was no place to get scared.

"Just look for clues," said Barry sensibly. "That is what we are here for."

Just as Barry said that, he looked down at his feet and saw something red. "Look!" he said. "A clue!"

Stooping down, he picked it up. "A red mitten!" he said. "It belongs to the ghost, I'll bet!"

"A ghost with only one hand!" said Spencer softly. "Wow!"

"He probably has two hands," said Robin. "He may have dropped only one mitten."

A little farther on, Robin stumbled over something metal. "Look!" she said, "I found another clue!"

She picked up the clue, and it appeared to be an old tin can.

"The ghost drinks beer!" said Spencer, pretending to put a can to his mouth to drink.

"It's not a beer can," said Robin, examining it. "It says FOLEY'S STARCH on it."

"It looks old," said Barry. "Look, it's all rusty."

"It is old," said Robin. "Starch doesn't come in cans like this anymore. It comes in spray cans."

She put it into her brown bag, along with the red mitten.

Spencer felt left out. He was the only one who had not found a clue. He decided to go off on his own to discover something to put in the brown bag.

After a few moments, he realized that he was

alone and did not know where his friends were. He lost interest in clues, and he headed for a small wall where he could sit down and think, when all at once he felt his feet go out from under him. He felt himself falling, down, down, into something deep. "Help!" he called.

Barry and Robin were busy digging through leaves and brush and hadn't noticed that Spencer was not with them. All of a sudden they heard a voice calling, "Help! Help!" It sounded weak and far away.

"The ghost!" said Barry, turning white. "The ghost is here, even in the daytime!"

Robin listened. "It's not a ghost, it's *Spencer!*" she cried.

Barry looked around. Sure enough, Spencer was not there. His voice was just barely audible.

"Spence?" called Barry. There was no response.

Barry and Robin called him together, more loudly.

After a while they heard a weak reply. "Come and get me," Spencer sobbed. "I fell into a pit!"

Barry began to panic. What if something terrible had happened to Spencer? This felt worse than when he had considered punching Spencer. His mother would really think they were careless if they lost Spencer in a pit in the woods! How would they find him? How would they get him out? Even if there was a doctor in the nearest town, how would he get to a pit in the woods? Barry knew doctors were not eager to make house calls; surely they would never ever make pit calls. And Spencer might have many broken bones. He might not be able to climb out, or to walk!

"Don't panic," said Robin, seeing Barry turn white. She called Spencer's name again. When he responded, she called loudly, "Keep calling our names. We will follow your voice till we find you."

"Barry! Robin!" he kept calling over and over.

"Good," called Robin. "Keep calling, Spence!" They walked in the direction of the voice. Soon it got clearer and louder.

"We're coming, Spence!" called Barry. "Hold on, we'll be right there."

"Over here," called Robin, running around a scrub oak. "I think he's this way."

They kept calling and answering, and finally

Spencer's voice sounded very, very close. But even then, they could not see Spencer.

"Down here!" he called. "And be careful, or you will fall in, too."

Barry and Robin ran toward a small wall nearby and peered over it. They could see the top of Spencer's head!

"Is anything broken?" called Barry anxiously. "Are your legs and arms broken?"

Spencer felt his arms and legs. "I don't think so," he called. "It's soft and mossy down here. But how do I get out?"

"I have an idea," said Robin, who was beginning to feel old and wise after having tracked down Spencer by his voice. "We will throw branches down, and you pile them up like steps. Then when you are a little higher, we'll reach over and pull you out!"

Barry felt like hugging his sister. That feeling didn't come too often, but right now he felt she was wonderful — and very smart. He had to admit she was smarter than he had given her credit for. If she could get Spencer out of the pit without broken bones and a doctor, Spencer's mother (please God) might never have to know how close they had come to really losing Spencer for good!

"Move over, Spencer," called Robin, as she threw branches and stones down into the pit.

Spencer piled them up as Robin said, and before long he was high enough to reach their out-stretched hands. He grabbed hold and hoisted himself up, using his feet to grip the side of the pit, just as he'd seen people on TV do to get out of traps. Here he was, Spencer Sims, a regular tele-vision hero!

Barry and Robin gave one last tug, and Spencer came over the wall. He brushed himself off, and except for a few scratches on his face and arms and legs, he was fine. Barry felt a surge of relief and a new closeness to his friend that only a brush with death can give.

"I'm staying with you guys from now on," Spencer said.

They all sat down on the wall to rest after their ordeal, and to plan their next move.

"What do you suppose this pit is for?" said Barry.

They looked at the wall they were sitting on.

Getting down on the other side and pulling the overgrown branches out of the way, they could see that the wall wound around the pit in a sort of kidney shape. At one end of the enclosure, they spotted water beneath some leaves.

"It's a pool!" said Robin. "A little pool for fish or something!"

Sure enough, Robin was right. The pit had once been a pool and a rock garden. And under more leaves they discovered a stone path winding from the wall through the woods.

"There are words on the stones!" said Spencer, down on his knees now, brushing dirt away. "Look, there are letters on these little tiles! I knew I should have a magnifying glass!"

Barry had to admit that a magnifying glass would be helpful. Spencer had been right. The letters on the colored tiles were so worn with age that it was hard to make them out. They scraped and brushed with their hands and fingernails, and finally they used the old mitten and tin can to help them.

"I knew it!" said Spencer. "This letter is an *M!* It is that *M* guy again!"

"Like on our silverware!" said Barry. "Let's

get the dirt off the rest of these letters."

They brushed and scraped for a long time, getting quite warm and dirty. But at last they could make out the name MILLER, one letter on each tile.

"Miller! The *M* stands for Miller!" shouted Spencer. "That must be the ghost's name!"

"There are more letters here," said Robin. "Before Miller!"

They scraped some more and made out the word FRANK and the year 1931.

"Frank Miller, 1931," read Barry. "This must be part of the old property. Our property. He had a fish pool way in the back yard."

"Spencer found this clue," said Robin. "It doesn't fit in the bag, but it's the best clue yet. Now we know the ghost's name, and 1931 must have been when he put the pool in."

Spencer was pleased that he had found a clue — the biggest clue of all.

"But we still don't know who this guy is, or how he can talk if he is dead."

"Well, he must be the guy who owned our house once," said Robin.

"But your mom bought it from Charles Finn," said Spencer.

"I'll bet," said Barry, "that Frank Miller owned it before Mr. Finn. I'll bet he built it."

It all made sense now. The only thing that did not make sense was the voice. Where did it come from? And how could a dead man talk?

Barry was still brushing off the stone path, and he began following it as he cleared it.

"Look!" he called, finally. "It leads right back to our house! Spencer was right. Frank Miller must be the *M* guy who lived here years ago."

"Well," said Robin. "We have a big clue now that we did not have this morning. We know the *M* guy's name, his whole name."

"Now," said Barry, "let's find him. Dead or alive."

Eleven

The Final Clue

After a little rest, Barry, Robin, and Spencer decided to go deeper into the woods, but to stay together at all times.

"Since we've already found this big clue, we're sure to find others in the woods," said Spencer cheerfully. Barry was glad that Spencer's misadventure had not dampened his spirits.

"Your clue was the biggest clue so far," said Barry warmly.

They forged ahead through the deep woods, finding only rare signs of human beings having been there before them. One was an old gray sock, full of holes.

"That looks too old to belong to our ghost," said Barry.

"Our ghost has been here a long, long time," said Spencer wisely.

"Yes," agreed Robin. "He frightened the Finns away, remember."

Barry put the sock in the bag. He had plenty of room for clues, authentic or not.

A little farther on there was an old tire, threadbare and shredded. That wouldn't fit into the bag, and they decided it was not a good clue, anyway.

After quite a bit of walking, they sat down to rest.

"We must be a long way into the woods now," said Barry. "Really deep, deep into the woods."

"It feels deep," said Robin softly.

The air seemed to press in on them, and it grew warmer and warmer since there was no breeze in the thick brush.

"I'll bet there is no person around here for miles and miles," said Spencer, his voice ringing clear in the quiet place.

"If we needed help, no one could come," said Barry. "We are really alone out here."

"Maybe we are too far into the woods to find any more clues," said Robin.

"That voice has to come from somewhere," said Spencer sensibly. "I think we should scour these woods till we find it."

Spencer's words gave the children a new zest for solving the mystery — they were investigators with a mission. It was up to them to solve this.

Just as they were about to stand up and move on, they heard a loud cracking noise.

"Was that you?" said Spencer to Barry.

Barry shook his head. They looked at Robin.

"Did you step on a broken branch?" said Barry.

"I didn't move," said Robin, her eyes wide with fear.

As they listened, there was more cracking of branches and the sound of someone walking, yet all three of them were sitting very still.

"Let's run!" said Robin.

"Where?" said Barry. "Where can we run to? There is no place to go."

The three drew closer together, listening.

"It's probably just a wild animal, a bear or something," said Spencer with a shaky voice.

"A *bear?*" said Robin. "I don't want to meet a bear in this woods. Where could we hide from him? He is probably hungry."

"It could just be a squirrel," said Barry. "Or a fox or chipmunk."

The noise seemed to grow fainter, as if it were coming from a distance, but just when they were gathering courage, it came back in their direction.

"Oh, boy!" said Robin. "This is it. We are going to be eaten alive. No help can get to us now."

The noise was now so close they could hear breathing.

"I think it is a person," whispered Spencer. "Maybe he has a gun."

"It could be a f-f-f-friendly person," stammered Barry.

"Who are you?" demanded Robin, in a sudden surge of bravado. "What are you doing in our woods?"

The breathing stopped. The cracking noise stopped.

"You scared him, Robin! Good for you," said Spencer.

Then instead of breathing and cracking of

branches, there was a bark. And then another, and then a loud series of barking very close to them!

Barry began to laugh. "It's a *dog!*" he said. "Someone's pet dog!"

"We don't know that," said Robin. "It could be a wild dog. Or a coyote. They bark."

As they huddled together again, a face appeared around the edge of a currant bush. It was a furry face with a spot over one eye.

When the rest of the animal emerged, they could see that it was a cocker spaniel with a wagging tail. He did not look wild.

"There's your man with a gun!" laughed Barry.

The dog put his head in Spencer's lap. "My mom says not to pet strange animals," he said.

The dog began to run about, nipping at their feet and acting as if he wanted them to follow him.

"I think he came to take us somewhere," said Barry. "He wants to show us the way out of here."

"I think," said Spencer, "he wants to lead us to our Final Clue. He wants to take us to solve the mystery."

"How could he know we even have a mystery?" said Robin.

"He knows," said Spencer in a sagelike tone.

"Well, I think we should follow him," said Barry. "He is trying to tell us something."

The other two agreed, and they picked up their clue bag and trotted off at the heels of the dog.

"Good boy," called Barry. "You show us the way."

The dog could run through the woods much faster than they could, and they had a hard time keeping up with him. Every time he sailed over an old log or a tangled vine or a small wire fence, they had to stop to help each other. The dog seemed to go through the thickest parts of the woods, where there was no sign of a path or clearing.

"Hey," called Barry. "Let's go this way. It looks easier," he said to the dog.

The dog paid no attention. He barked at them and ran the way he wanted them to follow.

"He seems to know these woods," said Spencer. "He's surely been here before. If he was lost he wouldn't look so well-fed and sure of himself."

Barry and Robin supposed he was right. Lately Spencer seemed to know what he was talking about.

"I sure hope he knows where he is going," said

Robin, wiping her face with a hanky. "I am getting hot and tired."

"I am hungry," said Barry. "Why didn't we take a lunch along?"

"We could have put food in our clue bag. There's plenty of room," said Spencer.

"We didn't know we would be gone so long," said Robin. "I never even thought of food."

After what seemed like hours, and just when Robin said she could not walk another step without food, the dog led the children to a large clearing. The grass was clipped, and flowers grew in a garden, and right in the middle stood — of all things — a house!

"Look!" said Barry. "In the middle of the woods! A house."

"That is where the ghost lives," said Spencer with conviction.

Barry and Robin laughed at him, and Barry said, "You and your ghost. Or your person with the *M* name. You think everywhere we go has something to do with him!"

Then Robin said, "This could be dangerous. Maybe someone mean lives here. Someone unfriendly or dangerous. Someone who hates children."

"The wicked witch!" said Barry, laughing.

"Let's just watch and see who comes out," said Spencer.

The dog had other ideas. He wanted them to follow him to the door. He ran in a circle around them, and then ran to the entrance of the house. As the three of them watched, someone looked out the window to see what the dog was barking at.

"Get down!" said Barry. They hid behind an oak tree.

"Look!" said Spencer. "It *is* a ghost! There is someone all in white in there."

They watched as a woman opened the door and looked out. Sure enough, Spencer was right. She was all in white. But she was not a ghost.

"She's a nurse!" said Robin. "Maybe this is a hospital, in the woods."

Barry was secretly relieved to find that he hadn't lied to Mrs. Sims after all.

The nurse called to the dog and let him into the house.

"Now what?" said Barry. "I am tired of watching and waiting."

"I don't care *who* lives there," said Robin. "I am going to ask them for something to eat."

"If it is a hospital, they must have food," said Barry.

"Who is going to go to the door?" said Spencer.

"We all are," said Robin, taking the boys by the arm.

They started slowly to the front door. The dog began to bark. Before Robin could press the doorbell, the door flew open. But it was not the nurse who opened it. It was a man they had never seen before.

He smiled at the children and reached out his hand.

"Hello!" he said. "Won't you come in? I am Frank Miller. Who are you?"

Twelve

The Mystery Is Solved

Robin caught Spencer just as he was slipping to the ground in a dead faint. When he opened his eyes (after Robin and Barry had shaken him a bit) he said, "I knew it! Didn't I tell you that the *M* guy would be around here?"

The three stood at the door of the house speechless — staring at the man who said he was Frank Miller. How could this young man be eighty years old?

Finally Robin said, "You aren't dead after all!"

Frank Miller replied, "No, as far as I know I am alive and healthy! Maybe you'd better come in for a bite to eat and tell me all about this!"

Not only was this ghost alive, thought Robin, but he could read minds! How did he know she was starving to death? Perhaps he was just hospitable, but he also must be very perceptive, she thought.

Inside the "hospital" in the woods, there was no sign of the nurse in white. The children sat on kitchen chairs and told the man the whole story of the voice in the night, and the M on the silverware, and the tiles around the fish pond, and the Finns' experience with the haunted property. They told him about the seance (and he laughed!), and how they had to solve the mystery of the voice in the night so that they could keep their land in peace.

The ghost looked very much alive as he listened and responded and opened the refrigerator and made the children very real chicken salad sandwiches. Then he poured them each a glass of milk and set a plate of homemade chocolate chip cookies on the table in front of them.

There was something ghostly and spooky about eating in a ghost's house, thought Barry, but he was too hungry to let it bother him for long. They finished all the food Mr. Miller had put out and thanked him. They explained how they found the house and why they came to the door.

"It was your dog who brought us here," said Spencer. The dog, whose name was Homer, sat beside Spencer and let him rub his ears.

Now that the children were not hungry, they thought of endless questions to ask Frank Miller.

"Was it your voice we heard in the middle of the night?" said Barry. "Were you telling us to get off your land?"

Frank Miller laughed. "No," he said. "I am afraid that the voice you heard was that of my grand-father. He has lived in this area all of his life, and now he is old and very forgetful, and we have a nurse caring for him. The trouble is, she works so hard all day long that at night she sleeps very soundly. Only a few nights ago, she discovered that he had wandered off. He may have been doing it for months, for all we know. When we heard about it, we came here right away, and we are staying the summer. In the fall we may have to take him home with us to the city."

"Then it was his voice we heard in the middle of the night!" said Spencer.

"I'm afraid so," said Mr. Miller. "He lived in your house many years ago. In fact he built it in 1931, and now that he is old, he sometimes thinks that he still lives there. We had no idea he was frightening people or haunting the land!"

Everything fell into place so easily now, thought Barry. In just a few hours all the clues had led to a solution. Their land was not haunted after all, and they could live there safely! And every time that Barry dried the silverware, he would see the *M* and think of Frank Miller! And not of ghosts.

Just then they heard a car drive up to the house. "Come and meet my wife," said Mr. Miller, "and my children. They have just gotten back from a trip to the store."

Children! thought Barry. It surely was an added bonus for the "ghost" to have children in the family! Today was certainly a day for surprises.

Mrs. Miller reached across a bed of petunias to shake their hands.

"Grandpa has been haunting their land," Mr. Miller said to his wife after he introduced them.

"Well, we hope to put an end to all of that," said Mrs. Miller with a smile. "Poor Grandpa thinks he is back in the old days again. He needs to come live with us."

"These are my two children," said Frank. "Carrie is twelve, and Christopher is ten."

Barry and Robin and Spencer could not believe their ears. Children just their age, living right next door for the summer. Well, if not next door, at least just through the woods.

Carrie and Christopher were happy to find friends their age, too. "We thought this was going to be a boring summer," said Carrie.

"Do you like to fish?" said Christopher.

"We love to fish," said Barry.

"And I don't think the summer will be boring," added Robin. "Before we knew we were coming here we thought so, too, but it turned out to be just the opposite."

"Maybe we can find another mystery to solve!" said Spencer. "I'm good at finding clues," he added.

Then they told the Millers about the tiles with the letters on them, and about Spencer falling into the pit and being rescued. In an hour they felt like old friends, and they had things planned for the following week.

"Just wait till Mom hears we solved the mystery!" said Barry.

"And finds out that we made new friends, too," said Robin.

"And that I was trapped in a pit and couldn't get out!" said Spencer.

Barry frowned. "Well, she doesn't have to know *everything*," he said.

"We would like to meet your mother," said Mr. Miller, when the children got ready to go. "After all, we have the only two houses on this side of the lake."

"Can you come for supper on Saturday?" said Robin. "My mom will be off work then and will have more time to visit."

"That would be very nice," said Mrs. Miller. "If it is all right with your mother, we will bring some fish, and we'll have a fish fry on the beach."

Barry jumped up and down excitedly. He had wanted to have fish for supper, but he had worried about cleaning them, not to mention catching them.

Before they left, they went into the sunroom to meet the "mystery" himself, the old Frank Miller. He shook their hands politely, and it was hard to

believe his was the voice in the night! He was surely not at all ghostlike or scary; he was a white-haired old man who was shaky and hard of hearing but quiet and gentle.

"Perhaps your grandfather can come along to our house," said Barry.

"Thank you very much, but I think he is better off here with his nurse," said Mrs. Miller. "He is so easily confused that it would be upsetting to him."

By the time they started home (Mr. Miller showed them a short cut) the sun was low in the west, and when they reached the house Mrs. Harrison was just driving in from work. They ran as fast as they could to tell her the news. But before they had a chance, she called, "I have something to tell you."

"Let her tell us her news first," whispered Robin to the boys. "Our news will take longer and we want it to be a surprise."

"It will be!" whispered Spencer, hardly able to keep the secret.

Mrs. Harrison put a bag of groceries on the kitchen table.

"Now," she said. "I want to talk to you."

Everyone sat down at the table.

"I have been thinking it over," she said. "And I don't think we want to own property that is haunted. I worry about leaving you here where we don't know anyone. And what would we do in case of an emergency? Something could happen . . . at night. I have not had any luck trying to solve the mystery, so I have put the house up for sale. We can move back to the city where we are safe, and Ace Realty will handle the sale."

"Now?" whispered Spencer to Robin. "Can we tell her now?"

The three of them looked as if they were going to burst.

"I feel so sorry that our venture had to end like this," Mrs. Harrison went on. "But you children need more friends, and you need to be in a safe place." She stood up as if the discussion was ended and began to prepare supper. She handed Robin the monogrammed silverware to set the table.

"Mom, we have news, too!" said Robin.

"It will cancel out your news!" said Barry.

"I was the one who found the best clue!" said Spencer. "Well, they helped," he added, feeling guilty for taking all the credit himself.

Mrs. Harrison looked surprised. She sat down at the table again. Everyone began to talk at once.

"We solved the mystery!" shouted Barry.

"There is no ghost!" said Spencer.

"We don't have to move at all!" shouted Robin. "There is no mystery, and we have brand-new friends our age to do things with all summer long!"

They told Mrs. Harrison the whole story, while she just sat in surprise with her mouth open, hardly able to take it all in.

"And they are coming here for supper on Saturday night!" Robin wound up. "You will meet them and see how nice they are and how we won't have to move after all!"

"We don't want to go back to the city yet!" said Barry.

Spencer shook his head violently.

"You did this all yourselves!" said Mrs. Harrison. "All yourselves, without my help!" she went on. "Why, you didn't need me at all! You did it all alone," she repeated.

"Can we stay?" said Robin. "Can we tell Ace Realty not to sell our house? We will have so much fun now with Carrie and Christopher!"

"Please, Mom!" said Barry.

Spencer was down on his knees with his hands folded, begging, just as he had done to his own mother when he had wanted to come with Barry to the lake.

Mrs. Harrison looked at Spencer (who had such a pitiful look on his face) and began to laugh.

"Of course we will stay!" she said. "I will take the house off the market tomorrow morning. And I can't wait to meet our new friends!"

Supper that evening turned into a celebration. Mrs. Harrison filled the wine glasses with soda and cherry juice and put a cherry in each glass. Then they toasted Spencer and his Final Clue, and their new friends, and the rest of the summer.

Then Spencer said, "I have a toast!" He held up his glass. "To our next mystery," he said. "We need a brand-new mystery to solve now that this one is over!"

Barry and Robin raised their wine glasses with soda pop to Spencer's toast.

"I think we have had enough mysteries," said Mrs. Harrison, who had not joined in the toast. "One mystery per summer is all we can afford."

But Barry knew that more adventure would come their way. After all, a few weeks ago none of them had known what was in store. Summer had begun quietly on their front porch in the city. And look what had happened since then! Real Adventure!

The same thing, Barry thought as he crawled into bed, could happen again. Only now there would be five of them to share it. And it would be five times as much fun!